Conditional Offer
Stewart Realty Book 6
By Liz Crowe

CONDITIONAL OFFER

First edition. May 5, 2024.

Copyright © 2024 Liz Crowe.

ISBN: 979-8224935420

Written by Liz Crowe.

Chapter One

Craig held the phone to his ear and let the cheap, fake leather office chair turn him in circles as he listened to his brother rant. Distracted, he touched the computer mouse. The screen flickered back to life, glowing in the cubicle's gloom. A bank statement was on it, reminding him how little remained of the money his father had left him.

He sighed and rotated the chair again so the motorbike showroom was visible through the wide expanse of glass. It was busy, but he had no energy for it. A familiar, unwelcome sense of boredom, coupled with mild panic, was gaining ground in his brain. He tried to focus on the words coming from the earpiece.

"You have got to go back to school Craig," his sister-in-law, Grace, took over the conversation. Married to his oldest brother, she was more like a sister than an in-law to him. She'd been part of Robinson's family life for years.

As the super-duper-surprise baby to an already large crew of boys, he'd had plenty of experience with the various girlfriends, and now wives, of his brothers, all big fans of well-intentioned advice. He sighed, tossed a tennis ball up in the air and caught it. "You're wasting your life there doing... whatever the hell it is you're doing."

"Selling, Gracie. I'm selling. Making a living. Drawing a salary, and a decent one. Did I tell you about my new gig? We're playing in Chicago in two weeks. At the—"

"Spare me the rock band bullshit. That doesn't matter either. I mean, it does, but..." She sighed in his ear. "Damn, your brothers ruined you, didn't they?"

The missed ball hit his leg. He watched it bounce away under the desk. "What? No. Don't be silly." He leaned forward, elbows on his knees, attempting to quell the restless energy that coursed through him. "I'm not that lame." But at that precise moment, he didn't buy his own argument. He put his hand over his eyes. Fighting the gloom that threatened his psyche, he did a mental switch-off so Grace could keep talking and he could toss out the occasional "uh-huh" and "sure" to placate her.

When they'd moved from his boyhood home in Louisville to Michigan so his father could take a big promotion at an auto company, he'd been the only kid left at home. He was the only one who experienced the not-so-special thrill of moving to a new town and a new high school in his junior year.

After finishing high school pretty much a loner, he'd been on a fast track at the University of Michigan in math and science, slated to graduate in three years. The youngest by far of five boys, his life had been paved with good intentions. But right now he felt like an utter failure, and it was tempting to blame his siblings and their well-meaning spouses.

As Grace filled him in on the latest from his rambunctious nephews, he pulled up a photo album on his laptop. There were zillions of pictures of his four older brothers, doting mother, and successful father. He could spend hours flipping through the virtual slideshow.

They were a large, happy family. Plenty of blond hair, expensively straightened teeth, various shades of tanned bodies abounded at the large family home on the east side of Louisville. He stared at the ones taken later at the Grosse Pointe, Michigan, house. The Christmases with the young men and their various girlfriends and subsequent wives, the big kitchen, pool, patio, all of it rendered in living color forever and ever, amen.

One photo made him lean forward and frown. He studied his father's smiling face as he held his youngest son. Craig figured he was probably about four years old—the year he and his dad started swimming together.

His grin was wide and genuine. He looked ecstatic. Because he had been. Time with his almost sixty-year-old father had been hard won. By the time Craig made his appearance, his parents left the bulk of his supervision to the small battalion of teenaged boys already in the house. When his father started taking Craig to the local YMCA in the evenings after the chaotic family dinner, they'd bonded to the point that Craig would forever associate the smell of chlorine and the bone-tiredness you got from a long hard swim with his father.

He'd been close to his dad, and treasured their time spent swimming with ice-cream afterwards every week. They'd avoided the usual father/son conflicts that beset his brothers and friends.

When Leo Robinson died from an aneurism in his office while Craig was halfway through his college years at the University of Michigan, Craig's entire world evaporated out from under him. He'd lost everything—his motivation for school, all of it. He spent a solid month in deep mourning. And now, he sold bikes, played in his band and watched his bank account dwindle—a real twenty-three-year-old success story.

"Damn it. Are you listening to me?" his sister-in-law yelled, making him flinch.

"No," he admitted. "Sorry." He leaned back in the creaky chair. A sudden flurry of movement in the showroom caught his eye. "I love you Grace. Tell Brian I'll talk soon." He ended the call and shifted focus to the smoking hot woman circling the Triumph Bonneville, a fancy-looking camera held to her face. His gaze traveled up the long line of her dark-denim clad leg to the curve of her ass. Her thin waist was covered by what looked to be a cream silk blouse that lifted and pulled delectably as she knelt and rose, snapping her pictures.

He smiled, relishing the shiver that shot down his spine as he stood and stretched. A colleague was making a beeline for her, but he stepped out, looked around, and slid in front of the guy. "Ah yeah, the magician," the other man said, patting his shoulder. "Go. Work it."

Craig rolled his neck around, shrugged his shoulders and shook off the loser-itis that had been gripping him. Grace's words were meant to motivate, but had only served to remind him of his failures. But he was fine. And he was about to do two of his all-time favorite things: sell a bike and nail a beautiful older woman.

As if reading his mind, she looked up, catching his eye. The sparkle there shot straight to his libido. Her full lips and high cheekbones screamed perfection. He'd guess her to be about forty, if not a tad younger. He took his time walking over to her, settling his A-game in place.

Anyway, he was bored. Getting laid, and good, by the woman about two feet from him would shake it all loose, sort him out. No problem.

"Taking pictures for your boyfriend?" He pointed to the camera in her hand.

"What makes you think I have one of those?" She tossed her hair back, making him bite his tongue to keep from licking his lips. He took a step closer into her personal bubble before moving past her, trailing his fingertips along the seat of the bike. The leather was soft under his palm as he put the machine between them. A small frown flickered across her face.

"Well, I would assume that someone walking around in broad daylight looking like you would have one. It's how it goes for guys like me." He turned the full force of his smile on her.

She tilted her head. "Jesus, you're cute. But I'm guessing you've figured that out."

He let himself have the blush, allowed the thick shock of his blond hair to drop over his eye and then brushed it back. A corner of her dark red lips lifted, mesmerizing him. "I'm Lindsay." She held out a hand.

He took it, lingering the right amount of time before letting go. "Craig," he said. "And this." He put his hand back on the expensive bike. "Is a classic Steve McQueen Bonneville. If you're considering it for yourself, I'm gonna ask now—will you marry me?"

Her light laugh sent a fresh shiver down his spine. She touched the leather seat. "Talk to me Craig. Convince me I should spend ten grand on a motorized bicycle."

"Well, first off, you gotta change your attitude about this machine." He put his hand near hers, close enough to sense the heat from her skin. "It's hardly a bicycle."

She leaned forward, giving him an unimpeded view of the tops of her breasts. He raised an eyebrow at her, forced his inner beast down under a layer of polite exchange. "The classic lines are only the beginning." He touched the cold chrome handle, let his fingers slide down to the fuel tank. "She is so very responsive. Both smooth and powerful." He walked around to the back and rested both hands on the leather, imagining the woman's hips under his palms in front of him.

"And when you red line her, I mean really bury the throttle deep?" He smiled when her face flushed. He touched her hand, moved away, crossed his arms over his chest. "When that happens, you know you've scored."

She threw her head back and let loose with a throaty laugh. Craig smiled and saw the line of salesmen across the back of the luxury bike shop watching him work. He shoved his hands in his pockets as he turned back to the woman. The fall of her inky black hair, the deep blue of her eyes, and the promise of what lay under the simple silk and denim she wore like a model made him take a deep breath.

"Okay, Craig. I think you need to take me for a ride." He let his smile linger as she leaned over the bike seat close enough to kiss him. "On the bike, I mean." She stepped back, tucking her camera into a case. "So I can get a sense of how much I can score."

Before he realized she could move that fast, she was around on his side of the bike. Her hand touched his shoulder, then moved down and caressed his bicep. He tried not to gulp. He didn't like feeling out of his league, and this woman was throwing off a strange predatory vibe about her that had a red flag waving in his brain.

"On the bike, I mean." She grinned, and her smile was sincere when she took her hand off him. He shook his head, cleared the cobwebs, and refocused on the task.

"At your service," he said, turning and catching the keys another salesman tossed his way. He grabbed two helmets and walked the bike outside. The woman's scent—a subtle, floral aroma surrounded by a clear spike of lust—was all up in his head, making him dizzy. His sales manager appeared by his side.

"Robinson, listen, the last time you did this." He lifted his chin to the woman who stood nearby, strapping on a helmet. "I didn't get the damn bike back for a week."

Craig put a hand on the man's shoulder, looked him right in the eye. "Don't worry, boss. I'll bring the bike back soon. I promise." He leaned in to the guy's very married ear. "I gotta ride this one out." He glanced over his shoulder.

The man's eyes glazed over at the sight of the walking orgasm, looking at Craig as if she was about to eat him alive. "Yeah. Um, okay."

Craig hopped on, fired up the engine, and let the woman mold herself against his back, her breasts mashed to his body, arms around his waist gripping his torso. He smiled, revved the engine, and took off into the near dusk of Ann Arbor.

Yeah. Get laid. That's the answer.

He smiled as her hand moved along his chest, then down. He put the bike through its paces on a four lane road all the way into a nearby town before he turned them onto the interstate, flooring it and letting the roar of the machine and the sensation of a lovely female against him block out all the noises crowding his brain. The messages from his mother, brothers and sisters-in-law about getting his act together and going back to school, the clear signals from his dwindling bank account, and the yammering of his own ego were an annoying cacophony. But the cool air whipping over his face and the feel of Lindsay's breath on his neck gave him strength. This was what he needed, period.

"Get off at State Street," she said in his ear. "Twelve eleven Pauline Drive. That's my place. I think we should take a break."

He nodded and drove them up the exit ramp. The sky was getting purple. Clouds scudded over the moon, and he felt like five million bucks. He was going to fuck this woman's brains out, and all was right in his world. Her hand hit his thigh. "You okay with that, sales boy?"

He chuckled and gunned the bike through the intersection, making her squeal and press against him in a most satisfying way. He let her whisper guide him, her hand moving up his leg and blatantly cupping his erection, as he steered the bike over South Main and past Michigan Stadium to Pauline.

It was almost full dark when they pulled into her drive and under an overhang, in lieu of a garage. He put the kickstand down and took off his helmet. Her hands trailed back up his torso and lingered over his shoulders. He climbed off and let the helmet drop to the concrete. His body was calling the shots, and he let it, happy to rest his brain that had been causing him no end of stress and anxiety. She dismounted, standing and letting her helmet dangle from her fingers.

"You said something about a break?" he whispered. He willed her to make the first move. As he expected, she planted her feet on either side of his and ran her hand up his arm, gripped his neck, but stopped, letting her lips linger.

"I want more than a break Craig," she said, her low voice making his cock even harder, which surprised him, considering. "No games. No bullshit. I want you." She reached down to unbuckle his belt. When she leaned up and bit his earlobe, he reached around her to grip her ass, sighing into her neck as she unzipped him and shoved his khakis down.

"Hmm... well, that might cost you extra." He cupped her breast, brushed his fingertip across one stiff nipple before yanking her shirt up. "I'm not that kind of guy."

"Really," she said, wrapping her fingers around his cock and bringing her lips to his. "I think you're very much that kind of guy. And I like it."

He licked her lips, stopping short of kissing her. His brain buzzed and his body tensed. He loved the buildup almost more than the act itself.

Almost.

"You have too many clothes on," he said, and unzipped her, shoving her jeans down before picking her up and setting her on the black leather Triumph seat, grateful for a lack of streetlights. He sensed her dark, lusty energy and wanted to taste it. Her breath was ragged as he dropped to his knees, running his hands along the slim musculature of her legs.

"That's it," she whispered as he licked his way up her inner thigh. "Somehow, I knew you'd be good at this."

She groaned as he licked her clit while sliding his finger inside her. Her hips angled, and she draped her legs over his shoulders, digging her heels into his back. Her smell swirled in his brain and his body took over as he sucked and finger fucked her to a loud, operatic orgasm. He stood, grinning when she wrapped her legs around him, tugging him into her orbit.

"Nice warm up, hot stuff." She sighed and threaded her fingers in his hair. He angled into her, let the head of his cock have full contact with the heat of her glorious pussy. "But I want more."

"Yeah," he said, leaning over her and grabbing the seat to brace himself. "Me too." He thrust hard, and let her low moan of satisfaction fill his ears and his brain. She grabbed his ass, met him thrust for thrust, but he held back, counting backwards from twenty, and mentally reciting baseball stats while watching her face.

There was nothing he loved more than the shape of a woman's lips, the look in her eyes as he satisfied her. And this woman—Lindsay, he reminded himself—was a classic multi-orgasmic example of exquisite older womanhood. She knew what she wanted and took it. And he was happy to be taken, if it meant quieting the unhappy noises in his head.

He spread his legs to brace himself and leaned over her to suck one of her hard nipples into his mouth, reaching down to stroke her clit. He'd lost his virginity to an older woman—a college senior—while he was in high school. She'd taught him a lot, and the string of older women he'd been drawn to since had only added to his knowledge and skill set, including the fact that women didn't climax from penetration. There had to be some kind of friction against her clit once a sufficient amount of foreplay had been achieved, and he knew just how to give it.

Craig pressed his thumb against that hard bud of her flesh and let her grip him as he pounded into her. She came just as he knew she would, long and sweet, dragging him with her. He grunted, and let go of the bike, trusting it to hold them up as they shuddered in each other's arms, their tongues tangled with a kiss. The gloom of dusk settled into night as his vision clouded over from the intensity

"Mm hmm," she sighed as he slipped out of her and stepped back, hands on his hips. "Just as I suspected." She leaned back on the bike, her hard nipples pointed up in the dark, her legs still parted and the glistening pulse of her sex shining in the moonlight.

"How's that?" he said, tugging up his trousers.

"Never mind." She giggled, hooking her finger in his belt loop and tugging him close. His brain was still foggy, but he knew he should go, take the bike back, and face his empty, lonely condo again—alone, to contemplate his unsure future. She palmed his still half-hard cock. He smiled and tucked her long hair behind her ear, letting her continue. "I think this should be an appetizer. To be followed by a full-fledged four course meal with gourmet dessert." She nipped his lower lip.

He started to step away. He really should leave. "I've been known to serve it up that way," he said, putting his arm around her shoulders.

Screw it. Or better yet, get screwed. Again, and maybe even a third time.

He tugged the bike into a dark corner, praying no one would steal the god damned thing while he stayed here and fucked this woman's brains into complete oblivion.

But she handed him a helmet, put hers back on and patted the seat. "Your place, lover boy. Take me there." He shrugged. Here, there, wherever, this was gonna rock.

Chapter Two

"Take 'em off baby. C'mon." Lindsay giggled and rolled over onto her stomach, gripping the camera. "You are just this side of photo shopped. Lemme see it."

Craig sighed, picked up his guitar and tried to ignore her, but he knew better. Lindsay was insatiable, and he'd spent the better part of the last three months as walking dildo for her. She'd rubbed his cock raw, but it distracted him from the constant mental reminders that he shouldn't be here, that he should be back in school. That alone was worth it.

He strummed and sang, and she snapped his picture non-stop. His phone buzzed on the table next to him, but he ignored it in favor of staring at the way her long black hair draped over her shoulders as she clicked away, keeping the camera between them.

He already regretted agreeing to a video camera in the bedroom. She'd come over to his place with it along with some of the most amazing pot he'd ever tried. They drank cheap wine, smoked, and had gymnastic sex that he barely remembered the next morning.

But after he'd stumbled over the camera the next morning as it sat blinking, ominous and a little intimidating in his quest for coffee, h"d stood, his body quivering, staring out the kitchen window, wondering how he got to this odd point in his life. Twenty-four years old, no college degree, making decent money selling motorcycles. Playing in a half-assed rock band and fucking a woman fifteen years his senior.

"Craig, sweetie," she said, rising from the bed in her full naked glory and running her hands through his hair, down his face, and settling on his lap. She set the guitar aside and slanted her lips over his. He drowned in her kiss, tried hard not to make this into anything more than sex.

He loved every single woman who'd taught him, who'd been drawn to him like bees to a bright flower. But he'd never considered himself attached to any one of them. Lindsay, however, made his whole body shiver and his ears hot. He wanted her all the time.

Love? Not likely. But it would do for now.

He smiled at her, stood and slid his shorts off, fisted her dark hair when she got to her knees and sucked his dick into her mouth. Groaning at the incredible sensation when she slid her expert fingers under his balls and stroked him there, then inched her way towards his ass. Unable to stop himself, his hips moved faster, and he grunted with the exertion of getting off yet again. He gripped her hair tighter as she kept up her exquisite suction, then her finger slid deep into his ass.

"Fuck!" he cried out, and pounded down her throat, furious at himself but helpless to stop. He came for what felt like an hour, groaning with the effort-slash-pain-slash-pleasure.

She released his cock with one last lick, trotted into the bathroom to wash her hands, then grabbed that infernal camera again. "Craig," she said in a sing-song tone. "Humor me?"

He ran his hands through hair. "Jesus. Whatever." He flopped down onto the couch and caught his breath, hearing the camera clicking but ignoring it. He plucked out a tune and sang, his voice croaky with frustration, using his guitar as a shield.

She climbed around him, had him sit up, move the guitar so it was just covering his crotch. She kept kissing him, running her hands up and down his bare torso, teasing his nipples to hard peaks, then backing off to take yet more damn pictures.

When she finally put the camera down and lit a joint, he tried to convince himself to make her leave. He'd never been to her place once in all their torrid time together. But had fucked her in every room of his condo, in his cubicle at the dealership, in the rooftop pool, after hours on top of another motorcycle in the dealership.

She held the joint to his lips. He took a drag, held it in, and then resumed playing. She climbed up on the bed, draped her arms around his neck as he smoked, played, and before he knew it he was naked, with a cowboy hat on his head, holding the guitar and doing whatever the hell she wanted him to while she snapped away with her infernal camera.

"You putting me on the internet or what?" he asked after she'd reached down to stroke him again. He grabbed her neck, forced his tongue between her lips, making her moan and mold herself into him. The emotion carried him as it always did. He understood his weaknesses with women. He'd do whatever they wanted, as long as he could get something beyond the physical in return. He doubted he would with this woman, but damn, she was addicting.

"You wish." She giggled as she pushed him back on his bed and straddled his hips. He yanked her down, pinched one of her nipples and kissed her hard, letting her get off on him, rubbing her clit against his still half-hard shaft. She moaned, pulsed and sighed, then sat up, her grin evil and infectious.

"I gotta tell you, I'm feeling used," he said, his hips already moving again, involuntarily, his cock pulsing with need but his brain shutting down, making him take her arms and ease her off him. She flopped over, frowning, but he rose, and made for the kitchen, ignoring her. This whole thing was making him insane, restless, and courting insomnia. He swam for hours, sold bikes, paid his bills and played music. Lindsay occupied his nights. He hated himself, and every day closed with him resolved to end it with her, only to find himself wearing her thighs as earmuffs within an hour of her showing up at his door.

• • • •

"HEY." HE ANSWERED HIS number two sister-in-law's call by rote, wondering how many of them were on the other line this time. "Sort of busy." He wasn't at that moment, but wasn't in the mood for their nagging.

"Craig!" Grace shrieked in his ear. "When did you start modeling?"

"What?" He half ignored her, one of three then-girlfriends who'd helped raise him. They'd coddled him, fussed over him so much he'd barely had to lift a finger to do anything for most of his growing-up years. Even after he went to college, they'd been at him reminding him to brush, floss, wash, wear condoms.

He groaned, determined not to blame the phalanx of women on the other end of the phone for his own lameness. He winced when he heard Brian's voice. His oldest brother was a successful engineer, had two kids and was married to the woman who'd started the phone call.

"Craig," he said. "The girls, they saw a ... a ... book cover. And, you, you're...."

"What the fuck are you guys talking about?" He rolled his eyes when Lillian, one of the still-just-girlfriends, took the phone.

"Sweetie, we didn't know you were modeling."

"I'm not," he said, anxiety setting up a distinct home base in his chest.

"Well, you're on a book cover. I hope you're getting paid."

"Holy shit. How do you, I mean..." He clapped his hand over his eyes, remembering that night, with the camera, and the guitar and the hat.

"Are you gay?" one brother blurted into his ear.

"No. I'm not gay." He opened his laptop, and pulled up a browser, immediately firing up a search engine.

"Well, your naked body is on the cover of a bestselling man-love novel. 'His Guitar Cowboy' is climbing the charts."

He tried not to yell. "How do you know it's me?"

"Your face, you numb nuts. Your pretty boy mug is there, along with your chest, arms, hands, guitar, and legs. We can imagine the rest, along with thousands of other eager readers. Seriously though, we'll support whatever sort of lifestyle you choose relative to your, um, sexuality."

"I'm a lot of things, Rick, but gay isn't one of them." He Googled the ridiculous book name, then tipped over backwards out of his chair when he saw it. He sat on the floor, staring at the improbable sight of himself, holding the guitar and hitchhiking on a country road.

"Craig? Hey? You there?" The voices of his siblings kept pouring from the phone. He hung up without another word, and flopped back on the bed, cursing the air blue.

Nice work Robinson. Not only are you on a gay book cover, you didn't even get paid for it. He set his jaw, sat, and turned the computer off.

• • • •

HE SIPPED HIS BEER and stared at Lindsay, attempting to keep his face neutral. The lightning from a spectacular storm still flickered, followed by the low rumble of thunder that matched his mood. "I hear I'm famous."

She looked up from her constant yet fruitless efforts at Sudoku. He always ended up grabbing the thing and solving it in about fifteen minutes. She set the book aside and put her feet in his lap. He ignored them.

She wiggled around, digging her toes towards his crotch. When he didn't respond, she rose to her feet and stood over him. He stared into her eyes, so as not to get distracted by her tits or her hips or any other damn thing.

"What the fuck is up with me on a book cover?"

"Oh, um..." She walked away, fiddling with her hair. He tore his gaze from her, realizing she was putting on a hip-sway show to distract him. "That."

"Last time I checked, I should get paid for stock photos of my image used on any public site." He sipped and attempted to stay calm.

He hadn't known this fact until today, when he looked it up. But he was determined to call her on it. She'd used him and made money off his photo. His photo was on the cover of a book, for crying out loud. While that didn't bother him, her using him and not telling him—or paying him anything—most definitely did.

"Lindsay, my family saw me on the cover of a bestselling gay romance novel. Please tell me you aren't shopping that video we took anywhere."

She kept staring out the window.

"Well, anyway, you owe me money." He stood, threw the empty bottle into the bin and glared at her. "And I need an answer about the fucking video."

She whirled around, her blue eyes snapping with fury. He met her halfway, gripped her arms. She leaned in, kissed him, but he pulled away, using every ounce of willpower he possessed. "I trusted you," he choked out. "I...love you." He had no idea why he said this, but once it was out, he couldn't take it back.

She laughed, and he stepped away, his face getting hot. "No, you don't. You love fucking me."

"Yeah, well, I did, anyway." He ran a shaking hand over his eyes and dragged a hard reality up from his gut. He grabbed another beer and tried to wrestle his temper under control. "But now I realize that you're a bitch and can get the hell out of my condo."

She swallowed hard, put her hands on her hips. "Okay, since we understand each other now." She grabbed her purse and started for the door. He sensed his heart shattering at the sight of her actually leaving. He squared his jaw, realizing just how played he'd been.

She turned at the last minute, giving him a final, teasing glimpse over her shoulder. He bit down on his tongue so hard it drew blood to stay quiet. He stood in the doorway, watched her hit the elevator button as she glared back at him. Then, before he could stop himself, he was at her side, shoving her up against the mirrored wall.

"Maybe I'll let you work it off," he said before slanting his lips over hers. She gripped his hair, wrapped her arms around him, and he sensed himself falling back down the rabbit hole, once again with his cock getting satisfaction and the rest of him becoming more and more detached.

"Hit the stop button," she muttered before pulling him into another kiss as she slid her panties down and off, then turned around to present her ass to his gaze and touch. "And take out what you think I owe you, however you want."

He stared at her, hit the button, then ran his hands down her sides, gripped her hips and tried to talk himself out of it. Lindsay was too much. He had to get away from her.

But she spread her legs wider, looked back at him through a curtain of black hair, with her hands pressed to the wall in front of her, and he was gone. The inane elevator music silenced, or perhaps it was the roaring in his ears, he unzipped and slipped into the warm sweet grip of her body. Leaning over her, he put his hands over hers and threaded their fingers together, moving his hips slowly, loving and hating it at the same time.

He pulled her hand lower, and they stroked her clit together as he moved faster and their breathy moans filled the small room. "Gonna come baby. Fuck me harder." Her voice lit a fire at the base of his skull.

He let go of her hand and let her keep rubbing herself, gripped her hips and did just that, coming loud and long as the room dimmed and brightened around him. They stilled, their breathing calmed. He slipped out of her and zipped up his jeans.

"Nice," she said, turning around and leaning back. "So, not mad at Lindsay anymore, lover boy?"

He picked up her lacy scrap of underwear and handed them to her, hit the button for the garage level and kissed her as an answer. When the doors slid open, he stayed put.

She ran her hand down his face, but at that moment, all he wanted was to get away from her. She was grabby, needy, and while his body valued her willingness to fuck him pretty much anywhere, anytime, he was getting uneasy about the whole thing. Not knowing anything more than her name, that she could afford an expensive motorcycle, and that he wasn't allowed to go to her house wouldn't cut it any more.

Despite all of that, he grabbed her hand. "Dinner tomorrow?" he asked as the terror of being alone that night overcame his disgust at himself for letting her continue to fuck around with him.

"I can't, my sweet. I'll call you." She turned and left him without another word.

• • • •

"MY MAN." HIS BEST CUSTOMER slapped his shoulder, making Craig want to punch the guy right in the nose, but he smiled and let the blowhard bullshit his way out of yet another purchase. The guy got off on visiting the dealership, loved to test drive, but bought nothing.

Craig half listened, stressing over the utility payment for the next month. He owned his condo, thanks to his inheritance from his dad, but he'd pissed away a shit ton of money on the band, his instruments, food, booze, and women. An embarrassing shit ton, and he had no idea where it went.

"You know," the dumbass kept talking. "You should try selling something where you make real money." He leaned back and put his feet up on Craig's desk.

It took all he had not to shove the asshole's dirty shoes back to the floor.

"Yeah man. Real estate. It is booming. One of my buddies is making a goddamned killing. You should try it. How hard can it be? You take a week-long class and a test, and you're good to go. You're some kind of genius, anyway, right?"

"Yeah," he muttered, trying not to remember his life as a successful college student.

"Not kidding, Craig. Look into it." The guy flipped a post card onto his desk, with a number and website, stating when and where he could take the class and the state-administered test. He picked it up, stared at it, then pulled up the website with a sigh.

Chapter Three

C raig shook the hand of the large-and-in-charge woman who was his new sales manager, grabbed a cup of coffee, and made his way into the conference room. He'd passed the real estate exams with flying colors, submitted his resignation at the cycle dealership, and still pined for Lindsay. Even though it was for the best, he was the sort of man who flat out hated being alone. But he'd been determined not to call her. And she'd answered his silence with her own.

He smiled at his new colleagues, ran his hands down his wrinkled shirtfront. He sipped, nervous energy consuming him while he looked around the room at the real estate agents whose ranks he had joined.

Then he saw her—Sara Thornton—the woman who would change his life.

She sat across from him, wearing a yellow linen-looking suit with a neckline dipping just enough for him to see the curve of her breasts. She was, in a word, exquisite. The sort of beautiful that he'd never encountered before, not even with Lindsay. His eyes narrowed, and the room and chatter around him faded as she scrolled on her phone and sipped her coffee. He could stare at her all day. The soft curls of her dark blond hair, the snap of her incredible green eyes and that laugh—dear Lord, he was lost.

She looked up, and he winked, leaned back, and crossed his ankle over his knee. His heart pounded so hard he almost turned to the guy next to him and apologized for making so much noise. Pam, the manager, introduced him. He held up a hand, looked over at her, the woman seated across from him, the one he'd already made a mental note to seduce, fast.

When the door opened, revealing a tall, handsome older guy in a flawless suit, Craig felt his newfound obsession wavering. The woman of his dreams seemed to disappear into that man's smile. He set his jaw and made a vow. He would have her, if for no other reason than to prove that he could, that she would find pleasure with him, at least once.

It was an old mental script. A familiar one. One he felt comfortable repeating, regardless of its viability.

He snuck another glance at the lovely woman and studied her as the man worked the room, caught his name and filed it away. Jack Gordon had everyone's full attention, of that there was no doubt. He realized with a jolt that the female vision of perfection across from him was doing her best to resist the guy. Her face was flushed, and she kept fiddling with hair. When Jack stood at the door about to leave, he shot a look so full of meaning at her it made Craig's skin pebble.

Yes, his new workplace was about to get interesting.

• • • •

"NO ONE WARNED ME THIS job was so fucking hard." Craig ran a hand through his hair and stared at the database he had built for himself, trying to rally everyone he could think of to announce his new status as seller of homes. Although he hadn't really pulled that off yet, either.

He'd taken calls, responded to emails and shadowed Sara for one day as she drove buyers around. But he'd been too mesmerized by her, too distracted to pay close attention to techniques with clients. He'd sat in the back with the male half of the buying couple and stared at her profile, obsessing over the tendrils of her hair curled around her jaw, and the way her lips moved when she spoke and laughed. By the end of that day, he'd been a horny mess. When Lindsay had shown up at his place, he'd availed himself of the opportunity, passing out right after from exertion, not even hearing or caring when she left.

His phone buzzed with a text from the office number.

"Craig, there's a walk-in," the receptionist messaged him. He straightened his tie and walked out to the storefront area of the downtown Stewart Realty office. Sunlight gleamed off the light wood surfaces, with all the flat screen televisions tuned to house renovation shows and sports. The hot chick at the front desk winked, then pointed to a thin woman sitting on the couch, perusing the listings on a tablet computer.

Within ten minutes of talking to her, he knew he had a live one, but her smile kept getting wider as she shifted closer to him with every breath. Her manicured hand landed on his thigh, making him jump. He looked at her—she was fifty if she was a day, well preserved, but he had more than he needed on his sexual plate between being infatuated with a woman at work and getting off most nights with freak show Lindsay. He looked up and caught the receptionist's eye, and gave her a "help me" look. She smiled and picked up her phone.

When Sara appeared at the door, glaring at him a little, he stood, holding out his hand and spouting bullshit about "life and business partner." They pretended to be a happily engaged couple for another hour until the prospective seller and buyer left. They laughed their way to the back office, where he sorted out her database problem, loving the excuse to be near her for any length of time. She was amazing, and it took all he had not to lean over and kiss her.

A few agents walked by, talking about an event they'd attended last night. An event where one Mr. Jack Gordon had been, and not with Sara, he presumed, based on her body language. She shut her eyes. He listened to the guys go on about Gordon and his hot date from some fundraiser, watching Sara's face redden.

He stood. This was one tangle he wanted no part of, although something in him figured he likely would be. He wanted Sara Thornton, that fucking uber-alpha male Gordon be damned. But it would not be today, so he backed out of her cubicle without a word. This Jack guy seemed like a class-A prick on a lot of levels, based on the office gossip that surrounded him and his womanizing ways. She'd figure that out and he'd be here, waiting to pick up the pieces for her.

Chapter Five

"Why don't I even know where you live?" Craig demanded that night, as Lindsay lay on his chest post sex. He ran his hand through her hair, then smiled at her when she flipped over and propped her chin on his torso. "I mean, really Linds, why so secretive?"

She stood, stretched, and started pulling her clothes back on. He put his hands behind his head, relishing his body's level of satedness, his mind half on Sara Thornton. "You deaf today?"

"No," she said, pulling her hair back in a severe up-do. "I'm just, private, I guess."

He enjoyed her rear view as she messed with her face in the bathroom mirror. "Maybe we should take a break from all this until you're ready to be less private."

She turned, her eyes flashing with something close to anger. Then she smiled and walked over to him, sat, and put her hand on his thigh. "Oh sweetie, there really isn't that much more to know. I love what you do to me. You love doing it to me. Why complicate it with details?"

Anger pierced him between the eyes and he sat, rolling away from her to the other side of the bed. He shook his head at himself.

This is not the woman you want. Let her go. Stop trying to engage her in anything more than sex.

But it wasn't in him. He wanted her around, or something like her, so he could shake off his newly found and highly annoying Sara obsession. "Fine. Go."

She walked around to his side of the bed and shoved him down, started to crawl on top of him, but he rolled away and stood. "I need to swim. Go on. Keep your fucking precious privacy, I don't care."

She kissed him before she left, but he kept it simple and non-committal. He yanked on his suit and headed upstairs to the top floor pool and swam for nearly two hours, blocking everything else out until he pulled himself up on the side, panting and about to puke.

He flopped down on a poolside lounge chair, drank some water, and then grabbed his phone. "Hey," he said when Lillian answered, rubbing his hair with a towel. "If I say you're my favorite, almost sister-in-law, will you tell me I'm not crazy?" She was the one he defaulted to most times. The other three were fine, but Lil was stable, tough and calm, a touchstone. Engaged to his youngest brother, she was the closest in age to him, the one who was the least inclined to suffer his bullshit, and he needed a dose of intolerance right now.

"Hey yourself, little bro. Sorry, can't do that. You're certifiable. Real estate? Jesus. You were gonna be a scientist, remember? Cure cancer or something?"

He groaned. "Don't start, please Lil. I need you not to nag. Just fill my ear with soothing sounds of 'Craig, you are the bomb.' Shit like that."

"Craig, you are the bomb. But surely the woman you are currently bedding can take care of telling you this."

He could hear some random kid noises. He had four nephews and one niece already and loved hanging around them. A sudden physical ache of homesickness swept through him. "I miss you guys."

"Move back then. You could sell houses in Louisville where a lot more people know who the hell you are. Why are you staying up there if you aren't going to school?"

A vision of Sara shot across his brain, followed quickly by a memory of Lindsay's face when he fucked her. "I gotta go."

"Wait, I have news."

"Oh?"

"We set the date."

"Oh. Cool. Congrats."

"Wedding is next fall. November-ish."

"Super."

"I love you, little brother. Be good. Protect your heart."

He sighed. "Will do." He hung up before he got more depressed, dragged himself back down to his condo and took a shower before falling dead asleep on the couch.

• • • •

SUNDAY WAS HIS FIRST real open house. He'd finagled a decent one from one of Sara's many listings. He wandered through the cavernous McMansion, running his hand over the granite surfaces, opening the doors of the gargantuan Sub-Zero fridge, admiring the expensive Italian marble foyer, cherry wood floors, and the kitted out man-cave basement. He put out his business cards and some brochures about houses of a similar price and style on the kitchen counter and waited.

He checked his phone, noting he had a call from his mother and some number he didn't recognize. He'd been avoiding Lindsay, hoping to wean himself off her and regain some focus. It did piss him off that she was so secretive, but he couldn't square his physical need for her with the nearly simultaneous urge to avoid her like the plague. He refused to entertain the concept that it was his own issue—that the fear of being alone made him keep coming back to her like a moth to a flame.

She drained him. Their every encounter was sexual, rough and many times angry, but she claimed to love it that way. He, however, was getting sick of it. She'd sent a text yesterday, telling him she was "available" for the night, but he'd ignored it and gone out to a bar instead. He'd flirted his ass off, groped some random woman in the smelly back hallway and left, brain buzzing and body unsatisfied. He could have easily brought the nameless girl home, but it seemed like too much effort for too little gain.

The doorbell rang. He straightened his tie and opened it, selling face fixed in place. The sight of Lindsay with her hair pulled up, dressed in a raincoat and high heels, set his body on fire. He gripped the doorway and tried to look pissed off. "What the hell are you doing here?" She stepped past him into the foyer, the patent leather heels click-clicking along the tile.

"Nice place, realtor man." She ran her hand across the mahogany banister. "Give me a tour?" She held out a hand. Even as he was shaking his head no, he had to observe himself as if from a distance, following her back to the kitchen. She leaned over the giant stainless steel island, pretending to study the view out the back window. His cock slammed into the back of his zipper. He reached out and yanked the raincoat off, revealing, not to his surprise, a corset, stockings and nothing else but those fuck-me heels.

Without a single word, he pulled all the pins out of her hair, letting it tumble across her shoulders. "Don't be so sulky, baby," she whispered, loosening his tie and pulling it off, then slipped it around her neck. She leaned back on the island, pressing her fingers between her legs. He licked his lips. "Lindsay misses you."

He grabbed her and flipped her around, bending her over the stainless steel surface. "Lindsay needs to not refer to herself in the third person." He forced her legs farther apart, making her squeal and shiver. "It makes Craig nervous and horny."

He bent over, whispered in her ear. "I'm gonna fuck you now, since that's why you're here." He angled his hips behind her and slammed into her nice and deep, whispering to her the whole time as she groaned and arched her back.

He grabbed her hair and pulled, reached around to finger her clit, making her pussy flex around him as her climax gained steam. She arched more, taking him deeper with every stroke. "Come Lindsay. Show me."

"Yes," she hissed and the contractions of her body yanked his own climax from down deep, making him groan and his hips move faster. "God! Craig!" she squealed. He pounded into her, filling her and cursing himself for not locking the front door.

Thankfully, no one showed up for the next two hours while they ended up sprawled on the basement carpet in an enthusiastic sixty-nine. He licked and sucked her pussy, only half realizing where he was and what he was doing. When she pulled her favorite finger in his ass trick, stroking his gland and deep throating him, he had a moment of Zen as his second orgasm of the day roared up from his spine and exploded down her willing throat. She pumped her hips into his face and came when he did. Then he pushed her off and stood, wiping his lips and staring down at the thin, sexy, forty-two-year-old cougar who'd been rocking his world for months. Without a word, he went upstairs, disgusted with himself.

She met him in the kitchen, sipping water and re-dressed in her raincoat. Something one of the sisters-in-law had said to him a few days ago floated across his still drug-addled brain.

"You need to settle Craig. As in, settle down. You're gonna be thirty soon and what do you have to show for it? No real job, no girlfriend, nothing but what your dad's money bought you in a town that's not even yours. Come home. We'll help you figure it out."

He clenched his fists, shoved them in his pockets and stared at Lindsay. "We are done. Do you hear me? Don't call me. Don't come over. No more open-house surprises."

She grinned and sidled over to him, ran her hand down his torso and put his tie back around his neck. "Don't be silly, sweetie. You'd miss me too much."

He jerked away from her, walked to the front door, and opened it.

She tried to lean in for a kiss, but he looked away and a bright shaft of resolve coursed him. He would cut her loose. He would prove he had a real job. Stop getting distracted by this woman and her manipulation and needy bullshit. She waved to him from the car, and he slammed the door, relishing the echo of it rolling through the empty foyer.

Chapter Four

Craig knew the day he become even further entwined in the Jack and Sara drama started out with him as a hero. He began the afternoon at his floor time shift by watching Sara jump in her car and head out to show a house to a total stranger in the middle of nowhere. He shook his head, trying not to be such a worrywart. After sorting through a whole lot of nothing in his email inbox and screwing around with his social media for a few minutes, he wandered up front to flirt with the receptionist. He contemplated asking her out, but stopped himself. He had a new goal now: less random pussy and more working towards a successful future.

He lingered as she leaned forward enough for him to get a splendid view of the tops of her tits. His sensed his newly minted resolve slipping when his phone buzzed with a text. "Hold that thought," he said to her, as he pulled it out of his pocket. He read the screen, tried to process it. 911—1750 Whitaker Road.

"Call the police," he shouted. "1750 Whitaker. Sara's in trouble." He headed out the back door like a shot, roaring down the interstate in minutes, fixating on the address, hoping he could remember how to get there, and praying she was okay.

He spotted her car in the drive first. As he roared up, he saw some redneck looking dude standing close behind her, too close. In the blink of an eye, the guy's hand was on her face, pressing it to the hot metal hood. Craig jumped off his bike, letting it fall to the ground, and yanked the asshole away from her, landing at least two punches before the guy dropped, screaming, blood pouring from his nose.

Rage blinded him as he jerked the attacker over onto his stomach, grabbed one arm and yanked it out of its socket. Craig couldn't hear much of the dumbass's blubbering and begging. When hands grabbed his shoulders, he shook them off, too angry at the dickhead whose shoulder he was standing on to care.

"Sir," a blue-uniformed police officer spoke, the single word breaking through his fog. His vision cleared, and he backed away from the still yelling attacker, letting the cop take over. Craig turned and spotted Sara, her blouse ripped and her knees shaking. He ran to her, catching her when she started to fall.

"Shh..." he soothed, as the adrenaline slipped out of his system, leaving him wobbly. "I'm here. It's fine."

The cops piled the guy into their car just as Jack sped up, spraying gravel from the wheels of his Stingray. He jumped out, still in full golf gear, and ran for the steps.

Sara stood and launched herself at him. He held her, closed his eyes, kissed her hair, then handed her back to Craig before stomping over and tearing the cops a new collective asshole for not letting him get his hands on the would-be rapist. Craig watched, somewhat detached, now cold and shaking himself.

"Sir, we need your statement." An officer not occupied with placating Jack stood in front of him. Sara sank back to the steps. He convinced her to let the EMTs check her out before giving his side of the story in short, clipped, to-the-point sentences, keeping his gaze trained on Sara.

Jack appeared, holding out a hand. "Thanks man. I'm told if it weren't for you..." The guy swallowed hard. Craig understood, even as a loud claxon of anger was sounding in his ears. He didn't like the guy, not one bit. And something told him he should walk away from this whole thing, fast. Get out from the middle of these two before it ruined him.

"Of course," he said. He gave Sara a one-armed hug and turned away from them, sensing the man's gaze boring a hole in his back.

Craig fired up his motorcycle, watching as Jack helped Sara into the passenger's side of his car, shut the door, then stood with his eyes closed for a few seconds. That moment—when he grasped the connection Jack and Sara shared but chose to ignore it—was one he'd look back on in the years to come. That connection was a brick wall he'd pound his head against again and again, realizing the futility of it, but unwilling to stop himself. The whole way back into town, he let a mantra play through his brain—the renewed focus he had on himself, which he was absolutely going to turn on her, and make her his.

. . . .

THE NEXT MORNING HE swam, as usual, although his knuckles smarted in the chlorine. He kept his brain calm, climbed out, showered off, and stared at his phone for a while. Finally, he pulled up a text Sara had sent him a few weeks ago that included her brother's name and phone number for "emergencies."

He hit the call button and put the device to his ear, blocking the voice that reminded him it was not his business, that none of this was anything like his business. That she was likely with Gordon. Of course, letting her make mistakes with a guy like that was part of his plan. Craig would be here to help sort it all out for her. He wanted her. So much so, it had become an obsession.

"Blake's in the shower. Can I help?" the guy who answered the phone said.

"Oh, uh, this is Craig. Robinson. From Sara's office. I'm, um, checking on her." He tossed a tennis ball up and caught it, deflecting his nervous energy.

"Oh, okay. I'm Rob. Blake told me about you. Sara's good. Home now."

"Oh?" he left the question unasked.

"Yeah, she stayed with Jack last night. Blake's apoplectic about it. The usual fucking mess with those two."

Craig frowned. The "usual fucking mess" comment threw him off. "Well, anyway, I thought I'd go by and check on her. What's your take on that?"

"Hmm, well, I've been Jack's friend for a long time, and I know how he gets. He may fuck it up a time or two, but nothing gets between him and what he wants. Fair warning, since you seem to want my advice."

Craig's words died on his lips.

"But," Rob went on. "If you go check on her, stop by The Local and have them box up a peach pie. She loves those. Good luck. You're gonna need it."

Craig stared at the phone for a solid five minutes before deciding it was worth a shot—yet one more fateful decision in a long string of them.

* * * *

WHEN HE GOT TO HER place bearing the pie, she answered the door huddled into a giant, ratty looking robe, devoid of makeup, her hair wet from a shower. He made his way to her cluttered kitchen and set the pie on the counter. She brushed past him before she paused. He was about to ask where she kept the plates when she started to tremble. He pulled her close, held on and let her cry it out.

She had his shirt bunched between her hands, her body pressed against his. He ran his hand down her hair, made soothing noises. Without allowing himself to think about it, he tilted her chin up, slid his hand around to the back of her neck, and covered her lips with his.

The kiss felt easy and perfect. She arched into him and had wrapped her arms around his neck when he broke the kiss and stepped away, not even sure why. He could have had her right then, right there. It was within his skill set, but it wasn't the right moment. He let it spin itself out, leaving them staring at each other.

"I'm sorry," he whispered. The doorbell rang, and she ran out of the kitchen, leaving him gripping the countertop. Kathy and Val from the office came in brandishing a wine bottle and pizza. They eyeballed him as she slipped to the opposite side of the counter. If there some state beyond awkward existed, this moment was one of them. He started to speak at the same time Sara said, "Craig just stopped by to check on me. Brought a pie." She pointed to the cardboard container emblazoned with The Local's logo. Both women looked from her to him, then back again, eyebrows raised in something between wonder and awe.

"Okay, I'm leaving you to your girl power session," he said, sounding like a total idiot. He clamped his mouth shut so as not to make it worse by saying any more stupid things, but stopped at the door, turned, and kissed her once more on the cheek. Her green eyes were so beautiful, he had to bite back a corny compliment. Instead, he went with honesty. "I'm not sorry I kissed you. Can I call you?" She nodded, flushed red in a way that made him have to remind himself not to grab her and kiss her again. He drove home in a daze, ever closer to his goal, but unsure of what he would do when he attained it.

Chapter Five

Craig looked around Blake and Rob's and wondered, not for the first time, why in the hell he'd come here. He'd been strong, staying true to his word on many fronts. Lindsay had begged him not to make her leave the night he'd told her to do exactly that, leaning on his closed condo door weeping and wailing until he threatened to call the cops. It hurt. He hated it when women cried, but she was playing him, so he held firm. After that incident, she'd left him alone, which convinced him of his original conviction about her motivations.

He'd gotten his first listing, and was presiding over his first successful buyer's agency transaction. Things were looking up, real-estate wise. But his obsession with Sara had taken on frightening proportions in his head. He used every excuse to be around her, talk to her, and loved how close their tiny workspaces crammed them together in the back of the downtown office.

She was an incorrigible flirt, which didn't help, but he worked it and listened to her rant and rave about Jack enough that he felt as dialed into that guy as he did to himself. But the memory of her lips, and her body, pressed against his, refused to fade.

"Come out Saturday to Blake and Rob's party," she'd said. "Allie will be there."

He'd rolled his eyes. He had gone out once with Allison from the Stewart administration office. A forgettable night and one he ended with a chaste kiss. She did nothing for him. Besides, he was bound and determined not to get into another meaningless physical relationship, unless, of course, that's what Sara wanted.

He'd accepted an invitation to the cookout at Sara's brother's place with trepidation. But now here he was, parking his bike, waving to a few people he knew, although there were plenty he didn't, and trying to blend in. He grabbed a beer, let Allie hug and kiss him, then chatted a while, ever watchful for Sara. He spotted her when she rolled up with Gordon in some obnoxious, over-the-top convertible.

She bounded up the steps to greet her brother and Rob. Craig observed Gordon sauntering up, noting the unfamiliar, pensive look in Jack's eyes. The man talked with a few people, including an attractive-looking red-head. Craig sipped his beer, letting the party flow around him.

Sara's brother and his partner owned a brew pub downtown. The tall one, Rob, was a French-trained chef, so the offerings were plentiful and delicious. Blake brewed on-the-nose classic styles, heavy on German lagers and pilsners, which Craig preferred. Two more beers in and he relaxed, but switched to water, knowing he had to make the trek back to his condo. A shout caught his ear. On impulse, he headed around the corner into the living room of the house, stumbling as Sara flew by him.

He wanted to grab her arm, but let her pass. Gordon followed her, his face a mask of frustration. On his heels came a tall woman who looked enough like Lindsay to make Craig blink until he realized it wasn't her. Intrigued, an ill-advised but inevitable protective sensation rising in his chest, he followed them.

Sara stomped down the steps. Craig waited long enough to note her brother's angry words thrown in Gordon's direction before Rob pulled him aside. Then he grabbed a couple of waters and found Sara sitting against a giant tree in the front yard. He crouched beside her.

Within fifteen minutes, she perched on the back of his bike, hanging on tight as he sped towards Ann Arbor. He had high hopes for the evening during the forty-minute ride to her condo. His body revved on all cylinders and by the time they got to her place, his mind was sharp, the rest of him more than ready. He helped her off, took the helmet and walked her to the door.

"Coming in?" she asked. She looked undone, miserable, and not terribly excited about having company. He forced himself to take a mental step away, admitting to yet another wrong moment. She loved Jack. What would he be but another tool, another boy toy in the life of a woman who didn't give two shits about him? Embarrassed, he looked up at the ceiling of the small portico over her door.

"What?" she asked, pulling his chin down so his gaze met hers. "Here's your shot, Craig." Her voice sounded sharp and unhappy.

"My shot at what?" he whispered. He sensed his well-controlled temper rising, pounding through him. He wasn't sure how to channel it. One thing was obvious—he had serious competition on his hands. He pulled Sara close, kissed her hair, but grabbed her hands when she ran them down his back to his ass. "No." he held her at arm's length. "Not now."

"Fine," she said, opening to door. "I get it. You don't want me. Jack can't stand me. I'm kryptonite."

He touched her arm. "Don't whine. It's a drag. You know damn good and well I want you. Problem is, so does he."

She cocked her head to the side and shot him a look that shot straight to his raging libido and pounced on it. He shut his eyes. "Don't," he said, stepping back. "I'll call you." He turned and ran down the steps without a backward look, his heart hammering, but his mind clear. He was going to win this.

• • • •

"I NEED SOME ADVICE," he asked Grace the next night. "Girl advice."

"Oh goodie," his sister-in-law said.

"No, I mean it. There's this woman and I... she's in a relationship, kind of, but he's an asshole and I... I don't know how to proceed."

"Take her with you to one of your gigs. Pull the rock star thing on her. She'll be a quivering puddle of goo by the time you're done singing. But..." she stopped.

"Not a bad idea. What comes after the 'but?'"

"We all know how you get. You fall head over heels at the slightest provocation. Don't put more weight into this one than any other."

He sat for a minute, contemplating her words. He was infatuated with Sara. Even though the more he saw her and Jack together, the more he doubted his odds with her. Still, that light-bulb style realization only ramped up his need, his infatuation, and he was starting to dislike that about himself, a lot.

"Yeah, well, so you're right again. Big deal." He was quiet a minute, and she left him to it. "I want her. Bad. I want to jump in with both feet and drag her the hell away from this guy, Grace. Cave man style. I'm... it's weird."

She laughed, and he relaxed. He loved his family, was grateful for all of them, even for all the spoiling and enabling of his innate laziness. "Craig Tyler Robinson," she started, making him wince. "You had better treat her right. You got me? Don't be an ass. Don't force her to make a choice. That will backfire on you. We taught you how to treat a lady. Now use it. And Craig...."

He stood and paced his condo, already contemplating how he'd ask her out and if she'd even go.

"Huh?" he said, realizing she'd stopped talking. "Sorry." He sat, knowing he was being rude and prepping himself for the lecture.

"Craig, honey. Please just... guard your heart. It's important to us. We're worried about you. Do you want to talk to Brian?"

"Well, I'm the little brother. So I guess you are stuck with worrying about me. And no, I don't."

She laughed. But something about the conversation was making him nervous. "Grace, listen. I know I'm being selfish, calling you all the time and stuff. How are Rick and Lil's wedding plans coming?"

"You don't really care, so don't ask."

"Sure I do. I mean, sort of."

"I gotta go. The boys are about to rip each other's heads off. Don't do anything stupid."

"Too late." He grinned. "And tell my nephews I'll see them soon and teach them how to get under each other's skin properly."

"I figured. Love you, little brother."

"Love you back."

Chapter Six

After Sara saw his band play for the first time, they laughed and joked their way through a late night Coney dog fix. In the parking lot, outside his car, he cradled her face and said words he would regret, but needed her to hear. "I have no intention of serving as a distraction, although I'm sure that would be fun," before he kissed her.

Because deep down, the more he got to know her, the more he realized that's what he would be. While part of him was willing to be that Jack Gordon filler for her, the rest of him—a maturing part — simply would not. Craig Robinson's M.O. didn't include holding back, either with his body or his heart, so he caused himself a fair bit of blue ball and heartburn pain. He'd never felt stronger otherwise.

• • • •

THE MORNING OF THEIR monthly Stewart Realty Company meeting dawned bright, clear and promising. No matter how strong his desire for the lovely Sara, he was damn proud of himself for being so mature. He was kicking ass at work, too. He'd closed two deals for his buyers, and now had a full pipeline of buyers and a few sellers. He sensed a sea change in himself—one that he would ride along with Sara, if she would let him.

He swam early, showered, and headed out on his bike. Since he didn't have clients today, the used SUV he'd bought to lug people around in stayed parked. He preferred the bike anyway and had plenty of months of forced separation from it in the wintertime.

The giant meeting room was packed. Jack was giving his first official all-company pitch and update for his downtown development. He'd done a great job on it. Taking a ten-year abandoned former newspaper building and gutting it for mixed retail and luxury condos was ballsy as hell right now, but that was one thing Gordon didn't lack.

"Save me a seat, running late," she texted as he poured a coffee, and noted Sara's brother standing at the back of the room. A bunch of downtown agents at a table with some free seats motioned him over. He put one leg up on the remaining empty seat. "For Sara," he said, feeling like a middle schooler.

He shot the shit, flirted, the usual, but was on edge the second he sensed Gordon nearby. The guy sucked up all the energy in a room without a doubt. Craig was getting used to it, but still didn't like it.

The room got louder, then quiet, and Craig looked to the back when the door opened, and Sara entered, surprising no one, as she was chronically late to group meetings. He smiled at the sight of her in a trim white skirt and blouse, her hair flowing around her shoulders. His resolve to ask her out this weekend, on a real date that would end with some real good times, hardened. He didn't want to wait anymore, but he had a weird vibe about the setup of this meeting. It was time to make his move. Now, right now, this minute.

She snagged yogurt and coffee and made her way over to the table. He pulled out her chair, enduring the funny looks. The entire company knew she and Gordon had been fucking around. Rumor had it they'd done it at an open house, in the hall of her office, and in Jack's office in the middle of the afternoon once. He had to hand it to the guy, given his own open house shenanigans.

The room dimmed just as Craig was about to whisper his date invitation. Jack made his way up to the front. He stood to his full six-foot whatever-the-fuck-it-was, smiled around the room, shot his cuffs, and pulled something from his pocket. Craig's heart pounded, but he forced himself to sit back, cross his ankle over the other knee and drape his arm over the back of the chair, prepared for whatever over the top drama he'd prepared.

He saw it on the screen and had to blink. Right up there where he expected to see floor plans, interior decorator renderings and pricing were the words:

"Sara Jane Thornton. Will You Marry Me? Jack"

The entire room sucked in a collective breath. Sara looked up, saw it and put her hand over her mouth. A quick flicker of frustration lit her eyes. When the entire room of one-hundred-plus agents turned to look at her, she smiled, and her face flushed. As she rose and made her way to the front, Craig stood, unwilling to watch any more, and walked out. His ears burned. His chest ached. Day late, dollar short. Figures.

Chapter Seven

Six Months Later

By the time the power couple engagement had run its course, Sara had broken everything off and Craig was an expert at ignoring the rumor mill. Blake called him throughout the early spring drama after the breakup. It was obvious Sara's brother wanted Craig to move in, to scoop his sister up and save her from herself. It was also infuriating, but he kept his focus, sold houses, went home and stared at his four walls. A lot. He jacked-off about the same amount because he was resolute. He kept his distance from his usual haunts—bars where he knew he could get picked up with very little effort. And he waited for Sara to come to him.

He swam more than usual and continued to ignore her, while his bank account grew since he was putting the full force of his energy towards the job. He even turned down band gigs, figuring it to be a more mature response. Whenever he played late into the night, he was useless the next day. And his business had grown to where he had to stay sharp every day.

The Stewart Realty summer picnic was the catalyst he never expected. There were stupid games where Sara and Jack got paired up and had to do crazy shit, like relays and an apple-eating contest. The horrific watermelon moment came when she'd had a slice of water melon between her knees and Jack was supposed to eat it faster than everyone else.

Craig's throat closed up with fury watching the spectacle. Sara's face reddened while Jack went to town, being his campy, asshole-ish self, considering he brought a date to the damn event. When he was almost finished eating the melon slice, Sara clapped her legs together, smacking Jack in the face and ruining their chance to win. Craig watched the two of them staring at each other during the near silence that followed.

Then she ran off and, of course, Jack followed her. The drama quotient between the two of them was mind-boggling and at that moment Craig knew he should avoid it. But he was worried about her, so he stood at the bottom of the steps of the house later, watched Gordon rushing down, leaving Sara at the top, her eyes full of furious tears.

He sensed his moment had arrived and seized it with both hands. He followed her to her car, offered to drive her home, keeping up his "hands-off, just friends" attitude, letting her lean against him. He sensed her desire for him to make the next move. But he didn't, and left her at her condo alone, although it almost killed him.

The following Monday morning he walked into her cubicle, right past that dickhead Gordon who kept hanging around the downtown office, invited her over for a swim and walked out was what he considered his Rubicon crossing moment. They'd had their official dinner date a few nights before, which had been weird beyond imagination since Jack had been at the restaurant, staring at them. They'd left the place, gotten ice cream, and he'd completed his long, long-term seduction at the end of the night by kissing her at the door—for real, and for a good long time—then walking away.

She was ready. So was he.

The pool was his venue, and he set it up well. She was a vision in her bikini, and they swam after he coaxed her in and gave her a quick lesson. The second he stopped in front of her up against the side and kissed her, allowing himself a deep taste of her, he knew it was all over for him. Their connection was erotic, but slow-building, and he'd been holding back for so long he had to concentrate on not blowing within seconds of stroking into her.

It took every ounce of his grown man energy not to tell her that he loved her, that he was the man for her. That she deserved more than Jack Gordon could or would ever offer her.

After the nice pool-side fuck, he convinced her to stay the night. When she grabbed him and forced him against the wall of the elevator as it carried them down a few floors to his condo, he groaned, and whispered it, just once, before she released her exquisite suction on his cock and rose, licking her way up.

"I love you," he said. Instead of answering him, she kissed him. As he pounded into her in the corner of that damn elevator, he forgot everything except her body and the feel of her legs on either side of his hips.

. . . .

BY THE TIME THE ENTIRE Ann Arbor real estate community figured out he and Sara were a couple, they'd set their boundaries. Ones he didn't want, but knew she had to have to justify what she was doing with and to him.

"Friends with benefits" sounded fine and hipster on the surface. By the time he figured out that she was with him physically, but in no other way, he was sick of hearing it. It sounded glib, flippant and a total dismissal of his purpose in her life.

The night it more or less ended for him, she'd been over for dinner. They'd mutually masturbated before the entrée, then fucked for dessert. He lay awake awhile, watching her sleep, trying to balance his need for her and his mounting disgust with himself for letting it slide into this bullshit corner—the place he'd vowed never to inhabit again but had somehow found once again. He slipped out of bed and fired up his computer and found his sister-in-law Lillian online.

Craig: You're up late.

Lil: Yeah, so are you.

Craig: So, I fucked up. I think.

Lil: The girl we discussed.

Craig: Yeah.

Lil: Sorry babe. Sometimes things just don't work out, I guess.

Craig: But I love her. I think. And she's here, asleep in my bed.

Lil: Dear God, are you serious? And you are on the computer with me? Is that legal in Michigan?

Craig: Shut up and listen to me. I wanted her, she broke her engagement, we went out, had a great time. And finally we... you know.

Lil: Yes, please spare me details of you having sex with anyone. Ick. I still remember you as a gawky ten-year-old kid.

Craig: Yeah, so...

Lil: Sorry. Go on.

Craig: She keeps calling me her fuck buddy, and we're all friendly and pals and in each other pants. And I want more.

Lil: but she's still in love with him.

Craig: Most likely

Lil: Oh honey.

Craig: Exactly

Lil: Listen, get out of that. You're just going to get hurt.

Craig: Too late. Thanks.

Lil: Ok. So time to disentangle. Let her go.

Craig: Easier said than done. I love her.

Lil: You don't

Craig: I think I do.

Lil: Craig, my adorable one, you love every woman you're with.

Craig: I do not.

Lil: Well then, let her go anyway. Suck it up.

Craig: I knew you'd smack some sense into me. I'm thinking about going back to school, btw.

Lil: Good for you.

Craig: So why the hell are you online at 1 a.m.?

Lil: None of your biz.

Craig: Oh yes it is. Is Rick being a jerk? It's within his skill set if I remember right.

Lil: Go, boot her out and go to school.

Craig: Yes ma'am, but I hear from one of the others that he's being a dick...

Lil: Yeah, yeah, whatever. Bye. I love you.

Craig signed out, stretched, then padded back to the bedroom. He jumped into the warm nest of sheets and Sara, holding her close and sticking his nose in her neck. Within an hour, they were awake and arguing the same old argument. He wanted more. She didn't understand why he wasn't satisfied with what she had to give. After she left, he fell back onto the bed, cursing his weakness and willing himself to let her go.

Her words rolled through him. "You don't deserve all my bullshit. It's why I'm leaving." He wanted to lunge at her, pull her back and beg her not to leave. When he recalled that they were due to go out the next night too, dinner with Blake and Rob, then a concert at the Ark, he groaned and pulled the covers over his head.

He wanted to cancel, protect his heart, make it a clean break, but he wouldn't and he knew it. Once again, he'd done it. He'd connected with an amazing woman, but hadn't been allowed in emotionally. It had to be some kind of record, the number of times he'd managed to do that.

Chapter Eight

He couldn't in good conscience get out of the dinner date with Blake and Rob even though it was obvious his fling or whatever the hell he'd had with Sara, was over. The whole damn thing felt so wrong to him now. He almost backed out. But the sister-in-law voices wouldn't let him do that—he didn't stand up a date for no good reason. The last argument with Sara passed in and out of his brain—her gorgeous, amazing face, contorted with frustration, his ugly words. All of it made his chest ache.

He kept it cool, and she played along during the first part of the evening, making small talk with her brother and Rob. The concert was great, but Blake and Rob seemed tense afterwards and when he suggested they get a beer at the other Ann Arbor brewery, the tension ramped up by a thousand. Sara put her arm around his waist and assured him it was okay, but the two men parted company with them on the sidewalk, leaving in an icy silence in their wake.

So they headed to the Big House Brewery, and he watched while Sara chatted with other beer drinkers, trying not to blurt out that he thought she should go back to Jack. The memory of her lips, her responsive body under his, and the hard reality that they had little more than a sexual relationship between them made his face burn with frustration.

He stared into the depths of the dark beer in his glass and counted to ten to calm himself. He'd come so far, had gotten Sara where he wanted her—in his bed, but that was all she had to offer him.

And it was bullshit. Here he was, yet again, in a web of his own neediness and obsession. He looked over at her, studied her amazing green eyes and gorgeous profile for the millionth time. When she turned to smile at him, he tucked a strand of hair behind her ear.

Bestie Craig had swooped in to pick up the pieces after the disaster of her broken engagement. But those pieces still had the mark of another man on them. A mark stronger than he'd ever imagined—probably stronger than she did too, since she spent so much energy denying it.

He sighed again, sipped and turned to face the bar, trying to figure out how he would deal once she went back to Jack. Sara touched his arm and spoke. "Hey Suzanne, let me introduce you to my friend Craig Robinson. He's an agent in my office."

He met the gaze of the redhead Jack had been talking to at Blake's party. Suzanne smiled at him and his heart sped up in a way he recognized, surprised at his reaction to her.

She was petite, her facial features distinct and lovely, even with the slight, silvery ghost of a scar that marred her upper lip. He took in her simple black blouse and found himself a tad breathless at the sharp contrast of her porcelain skin against the ebony silk.

He clutched his beer and ignored the semi-conversation the women had—Suzanne trying to get Sara to talk about Jack and Sara refusing to take part. When she touched his arm, he flinched. He took a breath and sucked in an intoxicating combination of malt and hops with an odd undercurrent of... something he struggled to identify. He leaned into her. And had to suppress a shudder when she met him halfway. "That's me," he said, realizing a response was required and going with what he assumed was still the topic. "Caught in the middle."

The women talked, or better yet, Suzanne tried to talk, and Sara deflected. As he observed their tense interchange, he found himself unable to stop staring at Suzanne. Her eyes snapped, and she talked with her hands as she tried to convince Sara—his date—to reconsider her rejection of some other guy.

Jesus.

It was surreal, but he wanted to reach out and touch Suzanne's cheek. To run his finger down her soft-looking skin. He blinked fast and refocused on Sara. His family's advice flashed across his eyes.

"Let her go. Suck it up."

Lillian had been adamant, and she was right.

He looked at the beautiful woman who owned the brewery, all five-foot-nothing of her but with a personality that took over the entire room. He had to force himself to close his mouth. "Uh, yeah," he said when he realized they were looking at him as if a verbal response was required. "So, what's your advice?" He dragged his eyes from Suzanne's wry grin.

"Don't know if that's a safe place, between those two," She gave his arm a squeeze and walked away. He watched her make her way through the crowd, then turned, embarrassed to see that Sara hadn't even noticed.

That night he lay awake, alone, and pondered the possibility of her—Suzanne, not Sara for a change.

· · · ·

HE SOUGHT SUZANNE OUT after that, showing up at her brewery's Tap Room more than once and engaging her in random chatter about her business. He was content to sit and listen to her for hours, he'd admit, and she got him talking, too. About his brothers, and the loser-ish sensation he was shaking now that he'd made some money selling houses.

One night, after a long, comfortable discussion and more than a few beers, he noticed it was midnight. They'd been talking, drinking and watching a Tigers baseball game on the west coast for almost three hours. He should go. But it was the last thing he wanted to do, period.

She leaned into his shoulder, startling him a little. "You'd better go home Craig." But she didn't move. He put a tentative arm around her. "Aren't you and Sara...." she started but didn't finish.

"I don't know anything about her anymore." The chaos that was his relationship with Sara hadn't let up. Regardless of his resolve to end it with her, they screwed and argued in succession on the regular, and he was sick of the whole thing. On the one hand, he wanted that supreme asshole Gordon to see him with her. To watch him kissing Sara, to imagine her in his bed. And that was wrong on so many levels. He was hard pressed to name only one.

Once again, he was trapped in an unhealthy relationship and didn't know how to disentangle. He suspected she was talking to Jack again, but knew they'd had no physical contact. His inner competitor kept forcing him forward, making him draw her even deeper into his life even though he knew it was for the worse for them both.

By now, he could touch her in three places and make her shudder from a quick orgasm. And God help him, he loved kissing her. Loved the little noise she made down in her throat when she molded herself against him.

But with Suzanne, things were... better. Relaxed and natural, not inclined to prove anything to anyone. He was turned on, as any man would be at the close proximity of an attractive female. But he didn't want to push. He just enjoyed her company. He leaning on the bar, beers in front of them, talking about nothing in particular. With her scent in his nose, a simple, comfortable stasis between them.

Suddenly nervous, he dropped his arm off her shoulders. She looked up at him, the dark brown of her eyes intense. "I should go. Sorry, I'm hanging around too late. Don't mean to be a stalker." He drained his glass.

She smiled, hopped off her barstool, and took their dishes around to the sink. He followed her, compelled and terrified all at once. Her compact frame seemed so fragile, so in need of protection. For all her bluster and big words about making her way in a man's world of beer, he sensed an inner core of vulnerability, and it brought out something in him he didn't recognize at first. A protectiveness that he'd experienced somewhat with Sara, before the whole thing turned into a contest, washed through him, making him shiver.

He walked to Suzanne and put his hands on her shoulders. She sighed and leaned back against him. "I hate being alone," he confessed.

He turned her around, brushed his lips over hers, and stepped back. Everything in him said "go forth and seduce" but for a change he listened to his bigger brain—the one that said, "Wait. Take it easy. You'll scare her away and you don't want that."

"You're alone a lot Craig, but you just don't see it that way. All that swimming—hours a day, you say. You don't get much more alone than that." She was quiet a second. "I like having you here. You're a good friend."

He ran a hand across his stubbled jaw. Exhaustion crept up on him. She went up on her tiptoes and kissed him again, let him feel the tip of her tongue parting his lips before she ended it, rubbing her arms and looking nervous. "You should go." She turned away. He hesitated, but after a few minutes, he slipped out into the night.

Chapter Nine

*T*ailgate Party - Michigan vs. Michigan State

Craig parked his bike a few blocks away in someone's yard in exchange for forty bucks and made the trek past the tailgating revelers over to the Ann Arbor Golf and Outing Course to an enormous party hosted by Arbor Title. He was tired after some late nights playing with his band and would skip the whole damn thing, but he'd told Sara he'd be here.

It was more of a sense of responsibility for her at this point, which was just as ridiculous. She was a grown woman capable of taking care of herself. He stood at the red light at the corner of Main and Stadium with the group of eager football fans waiting to cross and shivered with the memory of a moment shared with Suzanne the night before. How he managed to be here, in this situation, he had no idea. But last night had been amazing and not for the usual reasons.

"Hey," Suzanne said, looking up from her laptop. "What's up?"

He gulped, stuck his hands in his trouser pockets. He'd had a long, shitty day, full of deals falling through and seller clients on the verge of dumping him. His voice seized up, his throat was as dry as a bone. He looked at her, took in the jeans and a brewery tee shirt, tendrils of dark red hair curling around her neck. He ran his hand through his hair, consumed with uncharacteristic nervousness. She waited him out, her gaze neutral and expectant. Dare he say, polite.

"I, uh, thought I'd take you up on the brewery tour offer. You know, if you're not busy." He suppressed an inward groan at how lame that sounded. "Never mind." He sank onto a bar stool across from where she stood behind the bar.

She shut the computer, leaned on her elbows and smiled at him. His heart skipped a beat. Hot women intrigued him, made him want to flirt, impress and seduce. Suzanne brought out a different sort of Craig—one he didn't understand, and that scared him.

"Here." She handed him a beer and walked away. The sway of her hips mesmerized him, but he kept trying to force his A-game down under a layer of chivalry. One thing he'd never been around women was tongue-tied. Yet, there he was, smiling, and slamming down half the beer while she talked with the bar manager and put all her stuff away.

She glanced at him once, a puzzled look in her eyes. He shrugged, smiled, and forced his eyes up to the television and away from her.

After about fifteen minutes of messing around behind the bar, chatting with customers and other diversions, she was back in front of him, leaning in way too close for his comfort. He sat back, sipped more, and tried to ignore her.

"And so," she said, sipping water. "A tour, huh?"

"Yeah, well, you mentioned it last time, and I thought...." He should leave, escape the horror of his lame-ass behavior. But he couldn't. Not when she leveled that intense brown-eyed gaze at him. He had to clench his fists to stop himself from touching her hair, from pressing his lips to that sweet spot near her earlobe. He blinked. "Um sorry? What did you say?"

She leaned her head back and laughed, making him tingle all over. "I said you are too cute for words. If you want a tour, then follow me." She lifted the service arm and came out from behind the bar. He leaned back, unsure what to do now, but wanting more than anything to follow her. Something about her was so fascinating, so tempting, and so right. He smiled and grabbed his glass.

She stepped up into the brewery, holding up the superficial chain barrier between it and the Tap Room. He ducked under and listened as she launched into what was a well-practiced spiel. He sipped, looked around, and pointed to a glass jar of small candies. "Hey, are those M&Ms?" He walked over to a tall, makeshift worktable.

She followed him, putting her hand over his when he reached for the lid of the giant container. "No, Reese's Pieces." He looked at her, loving the warmth of her palm on his hand. "They're mine. I'm an addict."

"So give me the actual story here, Suzanne. I mean, you guys are successful, rolling in dough, expanding twice inside ten years. All is great? May I?" She nodded, so he lifted the lid and scooped a handful of the peanut butter candies.

She sighed and held out her hand. He put one chocolate covered morsel in it. She glared at him, ate it, and leaned back on a long, low stainless steel table. She seemed to relax, for the first time since he'd arrived, and drop her façade of a business woman in control. He gave her a few more candies. "It sucks sometimes, but I wouldn't do anything else. I love it."

"It sucks. And you love it," he mused, before crunching down on the chocolate peanut butter confection. "Damn, I haven't had these in years. I forgot how good they are."

"I know," she said, holding out her hand for more. "So, Craig, why are you here? You don't give a shit about my standard brewery tour."

He seized up a half a second, then grabbed more candy from the jar, dropping several into her outstretched palm. "How do you work here, anyway? With these things around all the time... Jesus." He popped a few more into his mouth.

She joined him, perched on a backless stool practically right under his arm. He wanted to move away from her, figured that he should, but then didn't. She took a few more peanut butter morsels and put the lid back on the jar. "I have to keep it stocked. That's the only rule. Because I eat the most of them, I guess. You gonna answer my question, or what?"

He draped his arm around her shoulder and they munched on candy like little kids. "I came to see you," he said.

She leaned her head against his chest. "I'm glad you did."

He startled out of the memory when someone jostled him from behind at the traffic light, and joined the cattle call crossing the street, ducking between the fences at the corner of the golf course. He spotted the giant yellow tent not too far away. Exhaustion stole over his brain, but he kept going. He was supposed to meet Sara. They were going to the game and then to dinner and then... he sighed, wondering what the fuck he was doing with her, anyway.

By the time he entered the loud tent, the party was well underway. He found some food, snagged a beer and leaned on the bar at the Big House station right next to one set up by The Local, Blake and Rob's brew pub. He looked around as he ate and drank while he sought her out—not Sara, but the lovely Suzanne. When she showed and they chatted, it was the most natural thing in the universe to be here, with her, laughing and talking. When she mentioned an ex-husband and money to invest in the brewery, he didn't push for the whole story. He'd never in his life felt such a need to go slow. Until now.

A commotion nearby caught his eye. It was Sara, arguing with her brother. Suzanne put a hand on his arm as he made a move towards her.

"I created that mess in some ways. I loved him. A lot. But he... it wouldn't work."

He stared at her a minute, then over at the argument between Sara and her brother. "And did he love you?"

"Yes. And he was crucial to my functioning at a shitty time in my life." She moved away from him, sipped her beer, and he sensed a barrier dropping over her — and between them. "But it had to end. So, I ended it." She touched his arm. "Go find Sara. She's in a tough place right now. Jack has a way of doing that to people. He's not a bad guy. I don't know how he gets himself tangled up like this, but...." She sighed and walked away without another word.

Craig finished his beer and followed the path Sara had taken. Unsure of what he was doing, why he was doing it, or what the hell he could do to help her. He took one last look around, seeking Suzanne without realizing it. When he saw her engaged in conversation elsewhere, he ducked outside, heard angry words, and faced the serious reality of the Jack/Sara connection as he stared at the women caught in a bullshit drama moment.

His eyes darted between Sara and Heather, the woman Gordon had been fucking around with since Sara had broken off their engagement. He heard her drunken and tearful accusations about Sara and Jack talking "every night" and how she, Heather, was with him in his bed, not Sara.

That tore it. He'd heard enough. He walked away from them, then turned and doubled back, his temper boiling, needing to confront Sara once and for all. Even as he kissed her, the words she said burned a hole in his brain: "You don't love me Craig. You love the idea of me not with Jack." She stalked away in the opposite direction from the loud party, leaving him standing, empty handed, heavy hearted and pissed as hell.

He ducked back into the tent, found a beer, then another, and another. Someone handed him a water bottle. He looked up and focused on Suzanne. She smiled, sat with him for a while and let him rant about Sara. Then after he'd downed three waters, she got up, keeping her hand on his arm.

"Purge her, Craig. She's Jack's. She always will be. I've known him a long time, and I can tell this is what is meant to be for them both. Do whatever you have to do, but get her out of your system."

She pressed a kiss to his cheek, and he stood, holding her close before she could slip away. He refused to screw up his friendship with this amazing woman by thinking he needed anything more from her. No way. Not this time. He needed a friend more than he needed a lover right now.

"Thanks," he whispered in her ear, and then turned away, hands in his pockets. He walked the six blocks to Sara's condo complex and sat on the porch until she showed up. She opened the door, and he followed her in, his ears buzzing and his vision blurry from too much booze and tension.

Their words were angry, hurtful on purpose, and when he yanked her close and kissed her, the fury remained. He should have left, but his body gave him different commands. His cock hurt it was so hard, and her smell, the lusty pheromones that were so part and parcel of Sara, made him dizzy. He heard her breathy commands, felt his hands ripping at her clothes. He kept asking her if she wanted this. Telling her he'd stop, even though he wasn't sure that he could.

"Don't be so fucking nice," she said.

She dropped to her knees and sucked him down her throat, making him gasp and grip her hair, the temptation to just blow so intense he almost gave into it.

"Stand up, god damn it." He pulled her to her feet, turned her around, grabbed her hips, and thrust into her. She was wet and ready, and that made him groan and break every rule he'd been taught—including one about always wearing a rubber. He had her mashed up against the wall. One of his hands gripped hers, the other was on her clit, determined that she'd come before he did.

"Harder," she commanded, her voice hoarse. So he did, without a single concern for her, but they were In sync on everything except the ability to go beyond that moment and he felt her pussy pulse and spasm in climax. The rest was a blur of angry words thrown and more rough sex. By the time he woke, almost falling onto the floor, he was so far from her side of the bed, his head pounded and his mouth so dry he could spit sand.

He stumbled into the kitchen and spotted his phone on the floor where it had fallen out of his jeans that still lay in a crumpled heap with her clothes. Embarrassment burned high and bright, making him wince.

Oh shit. He was not this guy. He had no business rough fucking her. She had enough going on and he didn't even want her anymore. She sure as hell didn't want him, and now he had someone else, someone calmer, someone more suited to him, on his horizon.

He squinted his eyes at an email on his phone screen and saw that a client he'd been courting had agreed to sign a listing agreement with him. So at least there was that, despite the steaming pile of shit that his personal life had become.

He found a pan and some bacon, then started the coffee before calling his brother to gloat a little over getting a primo listing out from under none other than Jack Gordon himself. When he felt a tap on his shoulder and saw the angry glare of the woman he'd treated like shit the night before, he knew it was the end of whatever beginning they'd shared.

Later that morning Craig sat in his truck, gripping the steering wheel, staring at Gordon's huge, perfect house.

Jack fucking Gordon. He screwed everything up. But did he? Or did Craig just drop into the middle of a shit storm and get buffeted around like everyone else?

He sighed, then put the SUV in drive and pointed it towards Suzanne. His need to see her, talk to her, to be calm in her presence was overwhelming. She did that for him, and he tried not to read anything into it. After that, he had to get to his brother's wedding in Louisville. His family was expecting him to arrive the next day. They sat, sipped coffee, she listened, and he left, feeling slightly better about his shitty behavior towards Sara.

The trip down to the wedding weekend was long and painful, fraught with bouts of hangover sleepiness and boredom. About three hours in, Suzanne called, the sound of the hands-free ring tone almost deafening him.

"Hey," he said. "Thanks for calling. Saves me from falling asleep at the wheel."

He felt like such a complete loser for the way he treated Sara. She was vulnerable and he went Cro-Magnon on her. A total loser move. But Suzanne had bucked him up, made him laugh. The sound of her light tone on the other end of the line lifted his heart like nothing else.

"You okay?"

"Barely. Talk dirty to me. That'll keep me going."

"Hmm. Maybe. That would mean I have to ponder the nature of our relationship."

"Yeah, well, ponder it into some 'what are you wearing,' sort of chatter, will ya?"

"Ok, how about this? Tell me about your brother. The one getting married."

He smiled at her deflection and humored her. "Rick is my closest brother. He was eight when I was born. He and Lillian are both lawyers, but she works in the public defender's office in Louisville and he's some corporate hack."

"Why is everyone down there? Didn't you guys grow up in Grosse Pointe or someplace?"

"My family's from Louisville. My dad was head of the big truck plant there. I grew up in Grosse Pointe because we moved to Michigan when I was a junior in high school—all my brothers were already out of the house. It sucked."

"I can imagine."

"I finished high school, swam, had no friends. Then I went to U of M for a year and a half on a three-year math/science fast-track program. I was going to medical school, maybe, or just getting a Master's and PhD in Chemistry. That was my area, I guess. Then my dad died, and I lost interest in pretty much everything." It sounded lame even to his own ears.

"Understandable. You were close to him?"

"Very." He swallowed past the lump building in his throat. The time he spent in mourning was still a dark hole in his memory.

"Sorry." She stayed silent for a minute. "You're pretty special, I think. I can see how much you care for Sara. I loved her brother once, too. It's a pretty crazy story. I'll spare you."

He frowned. He'd heard the rumors about her and Blake, remembered her comments from the tailgate party, but the guy seemed entrenched with his partner, Rob. Since Craig heard the warning in her voice, he let it drop. "So, about the dirty talk. Seriously, I'm hitting the wall here, sweetie. Throw me a bone, why don't ya?"

She laughed, and the sound was a balm to his aching psyche.

He shook his head and focused on her words, keeping the car pointed south. If he had to chart his growth as a man, he would start it with him as the center of the universe in a large, boisterous household.

His growing-up years were predictable, filled with the usual drama of a house full of teenaged boys but insulated by a father who made plenty of money to support them and a mother who was a fierce organizer, managing their many schedules and lives with alacrity.

Move to himself as a quickly maturing young man in high school, seduced his senior year by a former teacher and enjoying the hell out of it. He sighed and ran a hand down his face. Next would be the chaos of college, the newbie sensations barely overcome before the bottom dropped out of his world with his dad's death.

This followed by a long road of wrong turns, bad choices and mistakes, with Lindsay as the end of the screw ups. Or so he thought. But then came Sara, the culmination of his bad decisions. And now, Suzanne who was something different and special. He listened to her talk to him about everything and nothing, and he talked back until he pulled into the drive of his mother's house in Louisville.

• • • •

HE WATCHED HIS BROTHER get married, lifted his glass in toasts, and sat brooding through the reception. Various nieces and nephews ran around, tearing the place up as he got drunker and sank deeper into a slimy well of self-pity.

He smiled over at an attractive girl at one point, recognizing her from high school. Later, after a few dances and more drinks, he was pressing her into a corner, kissing her and imagining not Sara, but the small, perky redhead with the sad eyes in his arms.

After he'd made her gasp through a quick orgasm at the ends of his fingers and she'd rubbed him off behind some trees, they sat on the grass, passing a beer bottle back and forth. He hated himself more than ever at that moment.

"I'm sorry," he said, meaning it, "I shouldn't have done that."

The girl laughed and stood, pulling him to his wobbly feet. "It's okay Craig, don't worry, I won't stalk you or anything." She kissed him.

"You seemed so sad and you were never a sad guy. I thought I'd make you smile."

"Yeah, you did." He gave her that smile, squeezed her hand, then pulled the phone from his pocket. He sent one text to Sara, ending it with:

"Guard your heart. It's important to me."

She was headed to a fancy party to celebrate the opening of Gordon's new downtown building. Craig knew the guy would be ready for her. Jack would do anything to get her back, and Craig couldn't blame him one bit.

His next text was to Suzanne. "I want to see you when I get back. Take you out."

"Like on a date?" she shot back, making him smile.

"No, like on a polar expedition. Yeah, a date, you goof."

"Okay. I'd like that."

He shut off his phone, jumped up on the dance floor, and enjoyed himself for the first time in months. He sat with Lillian, Rick, Grace, and Brian at midnight, passing a champagne bottle around the group. His middle brothers, Travis and Allen, were already gone with their wives and kids. He pointed at Lil, the half empty bubbly bottle still in his hand.

"Tell me if this guy turns into an asshole, okay?"

"Fuck you, punk," Rick said, grabbing the bottle and taking a slug.

"Come home, Craig," Grace said, putting her arm around him. "Please."

He sighed, picturing the small, smart-mouthed redhead he'd talked to all the way down from Michigan. His phone had been hot to the touch by the time he'd pulled into his mother's driveway. But he would have talked more, just to keep her voice in his ear.

"Not yet. I think I'm gonna go back to school. I have another few months to use my 'get into Michigan free' pass."

"It's a girl, isn't it?"

"No. Yes. Maybe. None of your damn business."

"Is it that one, Craig?" Lillian asked. "The one that you talked to me about?"

"No," he said, pondering the reality of letting Sara go. "It's not. It's someone else. Someone... better."

Chapter Eleven

"Where's Sara?" he asked when he got back to the office two weeks later.

"She went home early. She's been sick."

A tiny alarm bell rang in his brain, but he ignored it in favor of trying to piece his real estate life back together and plan his next step with Suzanne. He wanted to take their friendship further, but her innate at-arms-length stance would take some time to breach.

After he didn't see Sara for another two weeks, his anxiety was off the charts. He'd heard she had gone to Florida to visit her parents, which was odd, but he tried to shrug it off. His attempts at still getting Suzanne to commit on a date weren't working, which kept him focused on that goal. Her continued excuses and deflections were beyond frustrating.

"Hey," a deep voice interrupted him. He looked up to see Jack Gordon dressed to the nines, as usual, staring right at him. He rose, his nerves on high alert. The guy looked haggard around the edges, but he oozed a pissed-off alpha male vibe that set Craig's teeth on edge.

"Yes?" he asked.

"I think we need to talk."

"I don't." He had to gnaw the inside of his cheek to keep from lashing out, but was determined to stay as cool as this asshole.

Jack leaned on his cubicle doorway. "Well, then I'll talk and you listen."

Craig stayed silent.

"I love Sara," Jack stated, shocking him. "And you need to back the fuck off."

Anger replaced shock, but he forced himself to continue the silence.

"That's pretty much it, Robinson. You got anything to say?"

Craig pushed himself up off the desk where he'd been leaning and stepped straight into Gordon's personal space. The man didn't back down an inch. "Yeah, I do. You need to become less of a supreme asshole if you think she's ever going to be with you in any significant way."

Jack glared at him.

His heart pounded. "That's right. Acting less like a selfish dickhead and more like a real man would go a long way to making her happy. Ever thought about that?"

"Sounds like you have," Jack said. The men stood toe to toe for a couple of seconds. "And I'm here to tell you right now you can stop thinking about her for any reason whatsoever."

Craig let his inner contrarian rule for a split second. "I am fairly certain that you…" He poked the guy's chest. "Are in no position to tell me what to do about anyone or anything."

Jack's eyes narrowed. "Out of my space, pretty boy," he growled. "And I'll leave you alone."

"Last I checked, you're in my space. So get your cocky ass out of here, before I…" His last words were drowned out by the sound of his own breath leaving his lungs in a whoosh. Jack hauled back for another blow to his gut, but Craig sidestepped him, landing a left-handed upper cut to the man's jaw. A couple of agents stepped in and pulled them apart before things escalated. Jack glared at him, but Craig's head was clear.

"I'm not who she wants. But by God, Gordon, you better man-the-fuck up and be what she needs or I will kill you," he said.

Jack turned and left the office without responding. Craig flopped into his desk chair, wincing at the pain from the other man's gut punch. When his phone buzzed with a text, somehow he knew it would be her.

Sara: I need you to come over. Now preferably. Fair warning Jack will be there too. I have something I need to tell you and him together.

Thirty minutes later he sat, stunned, staring at her, his brain reeling from the news flash. Jack stood and started pacing, throwing out questions. Craig had nothing to contribute, so remained silent. Of all the sex he'd had in his life, he'd never once even had a minor pregnancy scare, despite his aversion to condoms. He had an annual checkup for the usual nastiness and always came out smelling like a rose. His luck, he supposed. And it seems it had just run out.

When Sara's face drained of color and she ran to the bathroom, Craig followed her, no longer caring where Jack was or what he thought. He held her after she threw up, letting her cry for a few minutes. Once he had her settled on the couch, sniffling and waving them both away, he stumbled out to his bike. But he couldn't move. He just leaned against it, his pulse racing.

Jack emerged next, put on his oh-so-cool Ray Bans and started for his car. Craig glared at him, and as if sensing it, Jack turned and faced him, arms crossed over his chest. Craig shook his head. This was insane, beyond ridiculous. He refused to pretend her telling them both that she was pregnant, thanks to one of them and that she didn't care which one so they could just step off and out of her life, was in any way normal.

"That's a load of bullshit, you know that," he said, leaning back on his bike.

"Glad you figured that out." The other man said, mirroring his stance. "Now what, genius?" Jack whipped off his sunglasses. The expression of utter dismay, remorse mixed with regret fueled by pure smoldering fury on the man's face wasn't one Craig would soon forget. The urge to punch the jerk in the pie hole retreated.

"Yeah, she's a piece of work, isn't she?" Craig asked.

Jack sighed and ran a hand down his face. "You have no fucking idea, kid."

"Listen, we can't just let her do this. Keep you... us... out of it all."

"She can and she will. I, for one, am ready to let her, stubborn bitch."

Craig took a step towards him. Jack raised an eyebrow. "Look, skater boy, I'm not in the mood to punch your lights out again. So spare me."

"I don't care enough about you to bother hitting you again. But..."

"And the great unspoken words after 'but'?" Jack asked, slumping against his car again.

"But you and I both care about her." He pointed to Sara's closed front door. "So we, as in you and me, have to not back off. I know I'm not going to. Believe it or not, I'm not gonna let you do it either." Jack frowned at him, but he went on. "Listen, Gordon, I get it. You guys are crazy, in love, meant to be, whatever. I'm okay with it. I'll get over her." He crossed his arms. "You, my almost-friend, are gonna step up your mother fucking game with her or between Blake and me, we'll kick your sorry ass to Kalamazoo and back. We clear?"

His knees shook, but his brain was crystal clear. He thought about the cave of chaos he'd entered the day he met Sara Thornton, still mixed up with the whacky Lindsay and on the ragged edge of giving up on himself. But instead of getting lost forever, letting himself go on thinking he could beat Jack, take his woman away from him, Craig had met another, much more suitable woman. And she'd guided him down a side path, leading him into the light of day.

She still had hold of his hand. It was as if he could actually feel her small palm in his, tugging him away. As long as he wasn't a total dumbass, he could be with her. Which is right where he wanted to be. He took a breath, letting visions of Suzanne propel him.

"I'm going back to school," he blurted out. He had been toying with this concept since his brother's wedding when that very brother, in his disheveled tuxedo and drunk on champagne, had read him the riot act. It had solidified his wobbly resolve. He was going back and he might even revive the whole medical school dream. Who knew? He'd made some money and would keep his real estate license, but he'd been careful with his cash over the past year and had enough to get him through the remaining courses he needed to finish.

"'I'm going to be the General Manager at Stewart's," Jack said. "So we're both about to change our lives. For the record, kid," he said, his voice low, "my game is stepped up. I won't let her go through this alone as long as I can break through the wall of resistance named Blake."

"I'll handle Sara's brother. You're buddies with his partner, right? You work that angle. We'll make sure they both know we're here as back up, no matter what."

Jack shot him an ironic grin. "Good plan. Good luck with school. Oh, and by the way, you fuck with my friend Suzanne. You won't know what hit your sorry surfer-boy ass when Rob and I get finished with you. She means a lot to us. Never forget that."

Craig smiled, held out his hand. "Deal. And for the record, I'll welcome any bit of advice you guys have about her."

Jack took it, his grip firm but not overpowering. "If I can barely handle that one." He jerked his chin towards Sara's condo. "Trust me when I say I'm incapable of giving advice about Suzanne Baxter. Just... be careful. She's been through a ton of shit."

"Deal." Craig put on his helmet, climbed on his bike, and for the first time in his adult life, felt like he had a purpose. He pointed the machine towards downtown, eager to see Suzanne and tell her his new plan. Hell, he might even kiss her if he felt lucky. A hand landed on his shoulder. He looked up at Jack, backed off the throttle a little.

"Thanks, man." Jack said.

"No problem." He took off, his head squared with his heart but with the words "go slow" engrained in his brain for a good long time.

Chapter Twelve

"Wow." Craig sucked in a breath at the sight of Suzanne the night of their first proper date. She had on black jeans and a soft-looking cream-colored turtleneck. Her rich auburn hair was swept up off her neck and the look in her eyes was... wary. He took a step back from the door. "You okay?"

"Sure." She put a hand to her throat and seemed to draw into herself further. He needed to find out what happened to her that made her so skittish. But no one would tell him. All of them, from Rob to Sara and even Jack himself, insisted that she would tell him when she was ready. "Sorry. I haven't been on a date in quite a while."

He smiled and kept his distance. Something in her stance told him she wanted that. Contenting himself with looking at her a second, taking in her compact beauty, he waited while she shut the door behind her, and squared her shoulders as if girding herself for battle.

"Listen," he said, putting a hand on her elbow and ignoring her slight flinch. "Let's play a game." She shot him an odd look. "No, no, hear me out. Let's pretend this isn't a date. Let's say we're going to enjoy a musical performance, then share a meal and a beer and then I'll drive you home because it's more convenient to take one car instead of two — because I'm so into being environmentally correct and all."

She smiled, and his heart clenched. Oh crap. He was doing it again. Falling for an older woman. He kept his tone light. She elbowed his side. "All right, humor me. That's fine. But I get to decide at the end if we share a friendly kiss. How about that?"

Craig felt like a teenager on his first date as he opened the door and handed her up into his SUV. She stayed quiet during the short drive from her Barton Hills mansion to downtown. He looked for a parking spot, letting her keep her silence. It wasn't awkward, so he decided not to fill it with useless chatter.

"Thanks," she said as he came around and helped her out of the truck. "Tell me about this band we're going to see."

Relieved to have something to talk about, he gave her a brief history of the Paul Thorn trio, a bluesy-folk group out of New Orleans. They took their place in line outside The Ark, one of Ann Arbor's best places for live music. She leaned into him as he ran his mouth, and he put what he hoped was a casual arm around her shoulders.

No one, not even Sara, had made him experience this one hundred percent right-ness. He put his lips to her hair, closed his eyes a split second as the incredible blend of scents that were quintessentially Suzanne crawled into his brain.

By the time the concert was over, he realized he'd been staring at her in the darkened venue, admiring the way she sipped and talked to all the people around them. He gave himself a mental smack and refocused on being casual. But his body was sending him some serious "I want" signals he recognized.

He guided her out afterward, keeping a hand on the small of her back. As promised, they shared a meal, a beer, and he barely remembered anything that came out of his mouth or went into it. He was so damn lost in her by now. Her jokey sarcasm matched his but without lapsing into the brittle, like Sara's. Her energy was positive, slow-going, slow-burning. Unlike Sara's. She loved all the same foods he did, and he adored how she would go off on a tangent about beer at the slightest provocation.

He sipped his bitter ale and smiled at her.

"What?" She blushed and put a hand to her face, making his body react in an alarming way to the sight. He shifted in his seat. "I'm sorry, I go on sometimes."

He put his pint glass down. "You had me at 'alcohol by volume' but lost me at 'house ale yeast,' but I could listen to you read a menu, I think." He looked down, embarrassed by the admission. He jumped when she put her hand on his.

"Okay, so now we're on a date, it's pretty clear, and I have a question for you. It's kind of important to me, but I don't want to freak you out or anything." She stopped, picked up her glass, and he got mesmerized all over again by her lips as they caressed the edge, by the flawless line of her neck as she swallowed.

"Okay. Shoot." He swallowed, trying to regain his composure. Craig would look back later and realize that split second was the fork in the road for him. He wanted to follow her wherever she went and steeled himself for whatever tough question she had. It could be anything and he dreaded the "didn't I see you naked with a guitar on the cover of a gay porn book?"

"When are you going to take me swimming?" She put the glass down, put her chin on her hands, and batted her eyes at him.

He blew out a breath and sat back, trying to process it before he chuckled. "Damn woman, you know how to throw a guy off." He ran a hand down his face, leaned back further. "How about... now?"

He stood, threw some money on the table, and held out a hand. She slid her palm into it and he tugged her close, no longer caring what she thought about him being in her personal space. He planned to get even closer tonight. She looked up at him. "I'm about to initiate the friendly kiss," he whispered as the room shrunk to the two of them. "You good with that?"

She nodded. He touched his lips to hers. He kept it slow and light, determined to go at a pace she could handle, but by the time he heard the first cat calls of "get a room kids" from the other diners and a round of applause, she had herself wrapped around him so tight, her arms around his neck, her body pressed tight to his, and he was drowning in her. He broke away, but held her close.

"Okay. That's a good start."

She grinned and blushed again.

"I love it when you do that." He bit back anything more, let her go and held her hand all the way out to the car.

At the sight of her slipping out of her jeans and sweater and diving into the pool on the roof of his condo building in a black bra and panties, he had to will himself not to grab her and kiss her. So he suffered that teenager-ish feeling again as he joined her, shucking his own clothes down to his boxers before diving in.

After a few laps, she pulled herself up to the side of the pool, letting her legs dangle in the water. He rested his arms on the side and looked up at her. If he got out now, she would see the raging hard on he'd developed, so he stayed in the water, cursing himself for being such a damn kid.

"Jack told me about Sara."

He watched the water drip down her arms and held back the urge to leap up and chase it with his tongue. "Yeah. Um, that."

"It's a real mess. Sorry you got caught up in it."

"Jack and I have reached a détente on it. He loves her, and they can work out their shit without me."

"He told me you could be the father." Her gaze left his and looked out over the pool.

"I suppose. But she claims it doesn't matter. I mean, I care... but like you said. A mess."

He almost jumped out of his skin when she touched his cheek, then slid her fingers into his dripping wet hair. "You're a pretty special guy."

He smiled at her, but his heart was pounding and his cock was at full attention yet again at her touch. Any smart comeback dried up in his throat.

She bit her lip. "I don't know what to think about you, though. You're like a mystery. You just appeared in my life and I... I'm not in a good place right now."

"Hey, hey, hey." He hauled himself out of the water at the sight of a tear sliding down her cheek. "I do not make women cry. It's a rule that I feel pretty strongly about it." He sat next to her, put an arm around her and prayed she didn't see how tented his wet boxer shorts were. "You don't have to know how you feel about me yet. We'll just hang out, share meals and beer and keep saving the environment."

She sighed and tucked herself into his side. "I know one thing." She put her hand on his bare thigh, making him repress a shudder of lust.

"What's that?" He put his lips to her temple, sensing the slight pulse of her. "Whoa." He gulped when she flipped up onto her knees and straddled him, nestling her lovely heat against his aching cock.

"I want another one of those kisses. Like, right now." He leaned back, eyeballing her, trying to decide what she was really saying.

"Okay...."

She ran a hand down his torso, making his skin break out in chills. "I'm not ready for much more. Not yet. I've got some shit I have to work in my head, and I don't think I can handle a friends–with-benefits arrangement. It's just not in me." She bit her lip again. "I sound even worse for you than Sara. I'm sorry."

He leaned up, slid his hand around the back of her neck and brought his lips within centimeters of hers. "It's fine. We'll do this however you want." And when he kissed her again, it was fine. Epic and amazing and life changing, but also fine.

He stood, taking him with her, then scooped her up and dropped her down on the large lounge chair. They kissed until he was dizzy with a need for more, but he forced himself not to push it, to let her lead. Her small hands caressed him, stroked the outside of his boxers, but she sighed into his neck. They were both breathing heavy, and he had a horrific moment when he had to take her hand off him, kissing it and rolling onto his back. "Let's take it slower."

She propped on her elbow and stared at him. "Sorry." She whispered, touching his lips. "You really are amazing."

"No, I'm not. Well, yes I am, but I don't want to press you into doing anything you're not ready for."

"I'd better go." She stood and grabbed a towel. "Is there a place I can change?" He pointed to the small room and let his already supercharged imagination run wild as she changed, then reappeared.

This was going to work. It was good for them both. He needed this kind of relationship—one not so frantically sexual. But he knew one thing, and the sight of her running her fingers through her hair as she walked back out the door—he was in love for real.

And it scared the hell out of him.

Chapter Thirteen

Seven Months Later

Craig's head pounded, his body ached and his eyes burned as he held Sara's baby. Jack still sat at Sara's head, soothing her, brushing her hair back. The man's eyes looked haunted and considering what they'd all been through—a bloody mess at her office, the ambulance ride, and an emergency C-section—it was no surprise. His knees were shaking when a nurse finally took the baby from him. He stumbled out of the room, found a chair and fell into it. Suzanne appeared, and he'd never been happier to see anyone in his entire life.

Don't tell her. Don't say it. It's too soon. She'll withdraw.

He recalled the stupid night they'd almost connected about two months before. She'd brought dinner and beer to his place. He'd been unable to stop himself and had reverted to his old ways, had her on her back and was about to dive between her legs when Sara and her infernal pregnancy complications had torn him away, sending him racing to the ER because Jack had been out of town. Now, though, he was borderline grateful for that interruption.

He could stay his course and not rush her. No matter how damn horny he might be. They'd gone out to see movies, more live music, and she was a regular in the pool, doing her laps alongside him. He'd seen more of her body than he thought possible without having done much more than a near miss that one time. She held him at arm's length on all fronts, and he let her because if he were being honest, he loved being around her. Weird, something new for him, but he was going with it.

She put her hand on his knee. Her eyes were full of concern. "I'll drive you home."

In a total daze of exhaustion and depleting adrenaline, he gave Sara's mother a hug, shook Jack's hand, waved to Blake and Rob, and let Suzanne pull him out of the hospital and stuff him into her car.

He almost fell asleep during the short drive to his condo, opening his eyes only when she stopped in the garage. He hauled himself out, got in the elevator and tried to carry on a conversation. She slipped under his arm and held onto him. "Pretty intense. And you were the hero." He leaned his head back, ignoring how perfectly she fit into his side. He couldn't think about that now. He needed a shower and coffee. But really, he wanted to be in Suzanne's arms with no quarrel or fuss.

She woke him after an hour of being passed out naked on his bed. After spending almost as long under scalding hot water, be started to feel human. He put on sweat pants and a t-shirt, wandered out and found her in the kitchen with a fresh pot of coffee. "Hungry?" he asked, pulling out the ingredients for an omelet.

They ate, and ended up on his couch, feet up on the coffee table in companionable silence. He sighed, tilted her chin up, and looked at her. "I'm going to medical school. I already aced the MCAT and I've applied. I should hear soon."

"Wow. Okay. Quite the day for news."

"Sorry. Didn't mean to spring that on you."

"I'm not surprised. You'd be good at it. I started med school but didn't finish." He leaned back and stared at her, tightening his grip when she snuggled closer under his outstretched arm. "I don't have a pretty story Craig. I'll warn you now."

"Who does?"

She put her finger over his lips. "Shh... don't spoil it by talking," she said, cupping the back of his neck and pulled him close. The kiss was soft at first, before she got serious with it. He let his hands roam over her and she sighed, arching closer to his touch before she stopped with a bite on his lower lip.

She got to her feet, pulling him up. "You need to rest." He rose and stumbled to his room. His last thought before hitting the pillow was that he had never gone this long without actually having sex since he was sixteen years old, but that he was A-okay with it, as long as he knew he could see her again.

Two Weeks Later

"Well?" Suzanne asked as they drove over to visit Sara and the baby.

Craig glanced at her, smiling. "Well what?" He said, concentrating on the road.

"Well, what do you think about the state of the Chinese-American relations?" She smacked his leg.

"I think we should eat more Chinese food, especially that egg drop soup. Yum."

"Ass," she muttered, crossing her arms and pretending to pout.

He pulled into the driveway of Sara's small house and turned off the engine. After taking a long breath, he turned to her, once again blown away by the perky loveliness of her face, the deep hue of her eyes. He grinned. "I also think we should go out tonight and celebrate."

"What for? Sales of egg drop soup up?"

"That. And these." He reached into the console and pulled out two letters, one with the University of Michigan emblem and the other Vanderbilt University. Both began with the lines: Congratulations on being accepted to the medical school class of...

"You should go to Vandy," she said, after looking them over.

He startled. It wasn't the response he'd hoped for from her. "Oh?" He opened the door and climbed out so she wouldn't see the disappointment in his face.

"Vandy is an excellent school, Craig."

"U of M isn't exactly an online college."

"No." She grabbed the cookies she'd made, and they headed for the front door. "I'm sorry. I meant to say congrats. Well done." She stopped him, went up on tiptoe and kissed him. He tried hard not to grab her and shove her into the car, drive her home and show her what she'd be missing if he left for Nashville in a few weeks.

He settled for putting his palm against her face. "Thanks."

The door opened, revealing newborn baby and first-time mother chaos. Craig took over, held baby Katie as Suzanne sat and watched. He loved the warmth of the tiny girl against him, the bright look in her eyes.

After a while, Rob and Blake showed up with food, and Blake took over baby duty. Sara drifted off to sleep, and Rob carried her to bed. Craig crooked a finger to Suzanne, and she settled in next to him.

It was weird. No, it was surreal being there with the woman he'd obsessed over, thought he loved, now asleep in the next room with the baby that could be his across the hall. He sighed, pulled Suzanne closer and listened as Blake and Rob argued in the kitchen.

Craig had gotten snippets of the Suzanne/Blake story from Sara, but he still didn't know all of it. So yeah, this was a bizarre moment, all things considered. Suzanne sighed, put her hand on his thigh, and started to speak when the doorbell rang.

The circle of strange was completed when Jack walked in, still in his suit. He looked around, seeking Sara. But Blake was on a mission. And as the adults argued all around him about nannies versus daycares versus whatever, he began to drift. Suzanne poked his leg and he opened his eyes, grabbed her hand and threaded his fingers through hers.

"I have an announcement," he said, accepting the glass of wine from Rob. Suzanne raised an eyebrow at him but stayed silent. "I'm going to medical school. In Nashville."

Chapter Fourteen

"When?" Craig dashed off the text to Suzanne as he ran from his bike to the lab. They'd been trying to arrange a visit for months, and he was this shy of giving up, but something in him wouldn't. Something told him she was worth the effort. Like the work he was doing to achieve his goal of becoming an ER doctor, becoming the man Suzanne Baxter loved and trusted was challenging, but worth it.

"What about next weekend?"

He rushed in and sat, noting his entire group was in place already. But he smiled at the phone screen another half second before typing out a single word: "Perfect."

He conducted his lab, leading the group as usual, and dragged ass back to his bike, reminding himself he hadn't had a good swim in weeks. The slog of med school was proving way harder than he'd imagined. Plus, the building where he rented a studio apartment was full of a mix of medical and law students who partied at the drop of a hat.

He'd availed himself more than once of their hospitality. He'd slipped back into some bad habits, feeling on top of his game and surrounded by driven, smart people who worked and partied as hard as he did. But as much temptation as there was of the female persuasion, he never strayed, even though he sometimes wondered if "straying" was the right word.

One girl in particular had caught his eye. She was young, smart and hot as hell, so he allowed himself the odd flirt before drifting away from her. She was persistent and in two of his lab groups, so they got thrown together a lot.

He shook off the various frustrations, made it to the pool, swam for only one of his usual two hours, and sat on the side panting. His heart pounded at the concept of seeing Suzanne again. If she showed this time.

He gritted his teeth at the memory of the myriad excuses she kept making for never visiting as he took a shower, his head aching from hours of studying. Had he done the right thing? He'd lost count of the times he'd doubted it, considered dropping out, going back to Ann Arbor and picking up the real estate thing with the benefit of being able to see Suzanne every day again.

His family kept boosting him, brothers and sisters-in-law visiting, bringing him homemade dishes and excellent beer. He opened the fridge, found the latest Robinson-wife casserole and threw it in the microwave before pulling out his books and settling down for yet another long night of homework. Around midnight, while he was deep into his pathology book, his phone dinged with a text. He groaned, rolled his shoulders, and picked it up.

It was Suzanne. "Hey Sexy"

He smiled, and typed back: "More like ass-dragging tired and near brain dead."

Suzanne: "Yeah, year 2 is a bitch."

Craig: "So are you coming next weekend or teasing me yet again?"

Suzanne: "I'll be there by 4 on Friday. Be ready."

Craig: "Yes ma'am. Hope you're prepared to stay in bed the entire weekend."

Suzanne: "I am."

Craig: "Good because I need a fucking nap."

Suzanne: "Very funny."

Craig: "No. I'm serious."

Suzanne: "Fine, I'll plan some brewery visits so you can get your beauty sleep."

Craig: "No. You won't. I plan to greet you in such a way that you require a nap by Saturday."

Suzanne: "Ah. Well if you put it that way."

Craig: "I am. Putting it that way."

Suzanne: "Well, I'm going to bed. Get my rest before Friday."

Craig: "Good plan."

There was a pause, and he noted that the little icon indicating "Suzanne is typing" had gone away. He put the phone down, stared at it a while. He'd never in his entire life been this bone-deep tired. But his brain buzzed with energy at all the things he did indeed plan to do with her. After all the months of pleasant friendship, their polite companionship that eased into something else but never quite consummated, he was ready. He intended for her to be blown away by what he offered. He leaned back in his chair, put a hand on his hard cock, and stroked as he contemplated the ceiling. The phone pinged again.

Suzanne: "I miss you Craig. I didn't think I would, or rather, I tried to convince myself I wouldn't. But I do. And I can't wait to be with you."

Craig: "Yes, well, I'm told I am a bit like catnip..."

Suzanne: "I'll be the judge of that. And I'm like the Eastern Germany judge—I don't grade on a curve."

Craig laughed and stood, stretched, and shut the books for the night. He brushed his teeth, shucked off his clothes and got between the crumpled sheets. Then grabbed his phone and sent her a final text for the night.

Craig: "I hold gold medals in both oral and g-spot hunts already. I think I'll be ok."

He had his answer within seconds. "Ha. Well, I'll bring my score cards. Eat your Wheaties, young man."

He let thoughts of her fuel his fantasies, and after he came so hard he leaned forward from the force of it, he fell into immediate sleep.

• • • •

FRIDAY BEGAN BADLY. Craig's phone battery died over night, so the alarm didn't go off and he had to make a mad dash for his nine a.m. microbiology class. He took a huge exam in pathology, then slogged through a two-hour lab, enduring the less and less subtle attentions of the flirty girl.

He glared at her at one point. "Alicia, you need to back off, okay?" She blushed, and he felt bad for being a jerk. He put his hand on her arm, noting that she was one of the hotter women he'd ever seen. If things were different, he would have been between her thighs plenty by then. "My girlfriend...." He let the odd word roll around on his tongue. "My girlfriend from Michigan is coming down today for the weekend. Okay? I'm sorry if I sent the wrong message to you, but...."

She stepped back, her dark eyes unhappy. "Sorry," she said, flipping her hair and turning to the guy on her left. He shrugged, looked up at the clock and realized Suzanne would be pulling into his street right about then. He stood, grabbed his stuff, and jammed it all into his backpack.

"Later guys. Got a date." He jammed on his helmet, risking life, limb and speeding tickets in his haste to get over to his place. He'd cleaned it up the night before and hoped she wouldn't be horrified at how small the apartment was. While waiting a red light, he took a deep breath and let the reality roll around in his head a few seconds. They were going to be together. His body hummed with energy and he grinned like an idiot the rest of the way home.

He jumped off the bike, caught the damn thing before it fell over, and had to take a minute to catch his breath, shaking his head at himself. Her BMW was crouched by the curb, like an omen. He pulled his backpack up on his shoulder and walked toward the door, a strange sort of trepidation clouding his excitement. He opened the door, set his backpack down in the small entryway, and took a deep breath.

"Hey," he called, his voice croaky, which annoyed him. He had something to prove this weekend and meant to do it but anxiety about moving their relationship beyond what it had been for so long was humming through his nervous system.

Silence met his ears. He frowned.

"Suzanne?" He eased into the space that served as living and bedroom, with a miniscule kitchen, and bath over to the left. He thought he heard something there, turned his head and shivered when she caught her scent—a soft, spicy note with a distinct tang of brewery. Something about it made his anxiety worse. His heart pounded as he reached out to flip on a light.

"Leave it off." She sighed as she slid into his arms. Her lips met his just as he remembered, but something was off. His head wasn't straight. He kept the kiss somewhat noncommittal and pulled away, running his hand through his hair. A pure thrill of fear shot through him. He'd been with so many women, knew what it took to make all of them satisfied. But Suzanne was something different, and he had no intention of turning this thing into a sex-only arrangement. Although his body was sending him different signals—the message that said, "Yes, fuck her now" warred with his brain that urged caution.

"Sorry," he said, took a step back, and fell flat on his ass, stumbling over his own motorcycle helmet. "Shit," he blurted out, the sense of unreality overwhelming him.

She smiled and held out her hand. "Relax." Her soft voice calmed him.

He got to his feet without her help. "Sorry, I'm distracted, I guess. This med school thing is...."

She took his hand and led him to the small couch. "I know, believe me." He sat, leaned on his knees and tried to get his damn head straight. It kept spinning, and his body was like an exposed nerve, twitchy, horny and aggravated all at once.

She climbed around behind him, started rubbing his shoulders. "Like I said, relax. I get it." She leaned in and brushed her lips along his neck.

He shivered and moved away from her. She shifted with him, keeping up her massage. She dug deep, making him moan and lean his head back, but he was still nervous or something, and it pissed him off.

He got up and paced, then sat on the deep window seat, staring at her. She had on jeans and a soft pink t-shirt. He gulped. "You cut your hair. I like it." She grinned at him but he kept talking. "I don't want to fuck this up, Suzanne. And I...I'm afraid that we...." He couldn't even finish. He had no words. That was a first and did nothing to help his anxiety level.

She got to her feet and made her way over to him, conveying more in the few steps it took to reach him than in any conversation they might have. Her hips swayed, her eyes were bright. She licked her lips. "Craig," she said, her voice a soft whisper. She put one hand to his face, slid it around to the back of his neck, then ran her fingers through his hair. He closed his eyes.

"Look at me," she said, her voice firm again. The room narrowed. All he saw, all he smelled, and all he wanted was her. "I need you," she said, reaching up to put her other arm around his neck. "And I'm not waiting anymore."

Her lips covered his, her tongue probed. He groaned as she wrapped what felt like her entire body around him, pressing him back into the window seat. Her need was like a live thing, barely restrained between them. He shuddered as she lifted his shirt up and off, ran her lips down his neck, sucking first one, then the other of his nipples between her lips.

He reached out with shaking hands, ran his fingers through her hair. "Suzanne," he whispered, sitting back, paralyzed by this incredible moment. He'd spent years learning at the hands of experienced women and had become the guy who led, the guy who did the undressing and the initiation. But he was a limp rag doll under her hands. Except for his cock, which was so hard it made him wince in pain when she unzipped his jeans and yanked them down around his ankles.

He put his hands on her waist, loving the feel of her cool, soft skin under his palms. Something about that made his brain shut down, so he let go, leaned back on the seat and let her make her way down his shivering torso, until her lips found his shaft where she started licking, sucking, and teasing him. She stroked the skin beneath his balls, making him gasp and grip her hair, thrust into her mouth. She grabbed his ass with her other hand, encouraging him.

"Wait, I'm... God..." The orgasm hovered, ready to tip him over the edge. At the last minute, he called on his big-boy reserves, stopping it in its tracks. He gripped her arms, bringing her to her feet. "My scores are going down," he said as she lifted her shirt off, undid her own bra and stepped out of her jeans. "Damn woman, I'm..."

She put a finger to his lips. "You're perfect. Now, sit," she said, patting the window seat. "I'm feeling a little needy."

He shifted back, and gripped her neck, pulling her in for a deep tongue-tangling kiss as she got on her knees, straddling him. "Now," she whispered, breaking from his lips and making him want to whimper as she fisted his cock, gripping the base and making her slow way up to the head. "This," she said, pushing him back a little farther. "This is serious perfect score work." She lifted herself up, pressing the heat of her sex against his. His hips moved of their own accord. He grabbed her hips and pulled her down, trying not to groan too loud at the hot, wet grip of her.

"God!" she cried out, digging her fingers into his shoulders. "Yes." Her voice died to a moan as she slid up and down his length, teasing him by releasing his flesh, then enveloping him again. He leaned back in his hands, keeping a very tenuous control over the gut deep need to come.

She rolled her hips, found her rhythm, then leaned down to kiss his lips, his neck, to use her teeth and fingers to bring an exquisite bite of pain to his flesh. She kept whispering his name, rubbing her clit against his pubic bone and grasping the entire length of him with her pussy.

He sat up, changing his angle, and cupped her breasts, tugging at her nipples, watching her face.

"Oh," she said, her voice breathy again. "There he is..."

"Yeah," he ground out, planting his feet and meeting her thrusts as he captured her lips once more. He licked his way down her neck, loving the pure lust he smelled and tasted all over her. "Here I am." Her entire body contracted. She tipped her head back, calling his name over and over. They rocked together, arms and lips entwined and connected. Craig knew then—he would never, could never, ever let this woman go.

Their breathing calmed, but she stayed draped over him, her slight weight across his torso, pressed against his body. He held her close, kissed her face and neck while he attempted not to say what he wanted to say, knowing it would only make her recoil from him. He had to take this for what it was, and work as hard as he knew how to drag her kicking and screaming into the reality of a deeper emotional connection. She lifted off him and stood, reaching behind the couch for something. He opened his eyes, not realizing he'd closed them, and saw the card with the number 10 emblazoned on it.

"Fucking the Eastern German judge silly does wonders for my overall score," he said, standing and pulling his jeans up from around his feet.

She smiled, almost shyly, and what remained of his heart left his body and became hers. He pulled her close, kissed her, and then stepped away, determined to play it her way—keep it cool, for now. "Food?" he asked.

"Yeah," she said, heading into the tiny kitchen. "I brought some. Sit, relax, I'll feed you, never fear."

They shared bites of an amazing spicy gumbo with rice she'd brought, and slivers of fresh watermelon to cool their palates. He sighed and settled into the couch when they finished. "Damn, do you cook like that all the time?"

"Yep," she said, setting the containers on the leather ottoman and straddling him again. "Now, sustained by food, let's carry on, shall we? There are still a few heats left in this particular judging session." She threaded the fingers of both hands in his hair, tugging his face up to meet hers.

"Mmm..." he moaned into her lips, his hands finding the soft mounds of her breasts, the hard flesh of her nipples. Her smell was all around him, suffusing his senses. He had a weird drowning sensation, tried resisting it, then just sighed and let it happen before picking her up and walking them to the bathroom.

"Ow, shit," she mumbled around his lips when he cracked her head on the doorjamb, trying to get to the shower.

They soaped and rinsed off, giggling like kids. By the time he toweled her off, his cock was at the ready once again. He picked her up, set her on the edge of the bed and got to his knees, running his hands down her inner thighs. Then he stopped and flipped on a light. She sat back, her legs together, her face a mask of anxiety. He pulled her legs apart, noting the scars marring her flesh. They ran up one thigh and across her labia.

"What in the hell happened to you?" he demanded, his brain zinging with a fury he had no reference for. "Who did this?"

She reached over and turned off the lamp, tugging him down to her. "I'm not ready to talk about it yet. I will. In the meantime, I think you have a gold medal to defend."

She pushed him down to his knees. He gripped her hips, yanked her pussy to his lips and latched onto the small button of her clit, loving the sweet, spicy taste of her. That distinct, almost cinnamon-y essence that he would forever associate with Suzanne filled his mouth and nose. By the time he slipped his finger into her, reaching high and stroking her right behind the pubic bone, he came all over his belly without so much as a touch when she yelped, and grabbed his hair while her hips thrust faster.

"Je-sus," he groaned, licking his way up her torso. "Look what you did to me, you minx." He put her hand on his sticky stomach.

She sighed and leaned back, pulling him down beside her. "Sorry. Damn." She shivered, and he pulled her close, tugging the duvet up around them.

"I know," he said, kissing her neck as she turned and curved her body into his. "More to come, my love," he whispered, then dropped into the deepest sleep he'd had since starting school, keeping his arms wrapped tight around her.

She sat up once, her breathing ragged, and a scream on her lips. He jerked awake, disoriented and confused. Then put his lips to her cheek. "Shh ..." he said, pulling her back down. "It's okay. I'm here."

She sighed, letting him soothe her. There was more here than he knew, but he would wait, let her tell him when she was ready. "I love you," he said into her neck, grateful her soft, even breathing told him she was asleep and hadn't heard him.

When his-and-her inner alarms went off at five a.m., he groaned and sat, trying to get past the strange, almost hung-over feeling that possessed him. She wandered into the bathroom and shut the door, then back out, snuggling down into the covers and holding out her arms without a word. He kept his distance, anxiety tugging at his nerve endings.

"Tell me what happened to you, Suzanne. Please?"

She rolled onto her back, and the cover shifted, revealing a pale pink, erect nipple. He shivered as she spoke. "I will, but not today, possibly not this weekend. I was serious about having some work to do." She tried to get up but he rolled over and yanked her back down, covering her face and neck with kisses.

"Good, because I was serious about staying in bed all damn weekend."

She giggled and then sighed as he moved down her front, licking and sucking as he went.

Chapter Fifteen

Her next trip down didn't go as well. After the first time, he made a brief, unsatisfactory visit of his own back up to Ann Arbor, which made him wonder what in the hell he expected from her, ever. Other than wild, lusty snippets of time interspersed with maddening, long periods of miscommunication, she was hard to reach. And not just physically. She was distant, cool, flirty, as if he were something that amused her and nothing more.

His school commitments had ramped up to a point that he was wanted to mainline energy drinks for his caffeine needs. When she showed up as a surprise, in the middle of a party after a set of grueling exams, he wasn't sure what to expect.

"Hey, Craig," one guy said. He looked away from Alicia, who'd reinserted herself and her killer flirt muscle into his surroundings. He was so tired he could barely stand, but he leaned against the counter in the downstairs kitchen and let her work her eyelash fluttery, hair-twisting, somewhat mesmerizing magic.

The part of his brain that he allowed to think about Suzanne was cloudy with anger. He loved her and he knew it. It was real this time, not a passing obsession over a challenge to meet, another woman to please. He wanted to be with her all the damn time, and she did nothing to encourage it. The concept that it was the challenge that drew him anymore had taken hold in his brain and had settled in as a dull pain in his gut. This physical ache for her alone told him it was more than that.

"Dude!" The guy tossed an empty beer can at him to get his attention. It hit his temple. He looked up from his casual perusal of Alicia's tempting olive-skinned shoulder and saw Suzanne standing in the doorway still dressed in a cream-colored suit as if she'd come straight from a sales meeting. The men behind her gathered, appraising her slight form in the frank way only very drunk men will do. Possessive anger made his headache worse, and he moved away from Alicia, embarrassed by her proximity.

Suzanne stared at him. Her eyes touched only a moment on the attractive young girl still standing too close to be friendly.

She put her hands on her hips, making the guys behind her nod and poke each other in the sides.

"Surprise," she said, turning on her high heel and walking out.

The catcalls and annoying bullshit commentary that followed him out as he stumbled behind her made him want to punch a hole in something. But by the time they got to his top floor studio, the anger in her face matched his own. He felt a moment of relief. She had it in her to be jealous? Maybe there was hope.

He stared down at her, fatigue making him sway a little on his feet and his eyes go blurry. She glared at him as he opened the door, flipped on lights and stared around at dismay at the chaos that he called home. Books, laptop, phone, several sets of headphones, and notebooks all tangled up in a fine stew of empty pizza boxes, beer bottles, half-eaten apples and dirty clothes.

"Yeah, so surprises are sort of not my...mmmpf..." He stumbled back when she launched herself at him, covering his lips with hers, tearing at his clothes, then hers and forcing him back to the bed.

"Hold on, Suzanne, listen I... dear God..." He groaned as she slid his pants off, fisted his shaft and slid her hand up and down it as she bit down on his nipple. Her movements were frantic, and he met her halfway as the memory of those assholes staring at her perfection made a roaring sound in his ears.

He picked her up, tossed her down on the bed, and crawled up between her legs, licking and kissing his way up the insides of her thighs, trying to ignore the scars there, determined to have that conversation later. He flicked her clit with his tongue, slid a finger along the edges of her sex, loving that smell, the exotic spicy essence she seemed to emanate when aroused.

She reached down and pulled him up, arching her body into his. "Hold on," he tried to stop, but she wrapped her legs around his waist and angled herself so he could stroke into her, deep, moaning with repressed loneliness, and a year of pure horny fueled only by a bit of phone sex and plenty of argument.

"Craig," she said, cradling his face as their bodies moved slowly but with purpose.

"Hmm?" He leaned down to lap at her nipples, loving the taste of her all over again.

"I'm sorry. I shouldn't have surprised you and I should be a better talker, open up to more but I...oh..." He shifted forward, bringing her clit in direct contact with his pubic bone as he continued to roll one of her nipples between his fingers. He moved faster, needing something, something more than the simple pleasure of a physical release.

"Surprise me anytime, as long as we can do this." But he knew this wasn't the answer for them. They had miles to go to overcome their barriers. As she came in a glorious burst of erotic energy, contracting around him so hard he joined her, their cries of pleasure mixing in the small, overheated room. It was all he needed. He dropped to his side, the exhaustion and rush of hormones making him so sleepy he slurred his words. "C'mere. Sleep with me. Please."

She smiled and kissed his nose. "I can only stay one night. But yes, I will sleep with you Craig. I...."

As the fog of exhaustion overtook him, he heard it, and tried to struggle awake, but the last months' and that night's intensities plowed him under. "I love you," she whispered, as she lay across him.

The next morning, he woke to the sound of a shower and the smell of coffee. He groaned and rolled over, groping the bed for her, but of course, she was gone. His body was rock hard again, and he needed to connect with her once more, hoped to hear words he thought he dreamed the night before. She emerged, dressed in a different suit, holding two cups of coffee and a wearing a satisfied smile.

A strange sort of anger washed over him, and he opened his mouth before thinking. "Glad I could help you out. Scratch that itch or whatever. Be sure and leave the money on the table."

She looked puzzled for a second, and then a matching fury lit her eyes. She set the coffee mugs down. "That's what you think? Why I came down here?"

"Why else?" He put his arms behind his head and let stupid shit pour from him without stopping it. "You came, you got off, now you leave, dressed to kill, or sell, or whatever it is you're here for besides fucking the med student."

She straightened her shoulders and a neutral look slipped over her face. He sat up, tried to get the moment back, but it was way too late.

"I came here to see you, be with you, and have sex, yes, but you seemed pretty in tune with that program. Sorry if you feel violated."

"No, I..." His head started pounding again. "Shit."

"Yeah. I'm going." She started for the door.

He leapt up, grabbed her arm. "You told me you loved me last night. I heard it."

She glanced down at the hand he had wrapped around her bicep. He let go and stepped back. She crossed her arms and leveled a look at him that made his chest ache. "Maybe so, Craig. And if your asshole behavior this morning is any indication, I've made a mistake admitting it. Good bye."

"No, wait," he yelled, but it only came out a whisper and he dropped into a chair, put his head on his arms and cursed himself for a solid thirty minutes before letting the bright burn of anger take over.

Who the fuck did she think she was? She had done nothing but mess with his head for... what... three years? Screw that, screw her issues and complications and whatever shit went down in her past that she wouldn't share with him.

His hands shook as he grabbed his phone, found the contact labeled: "Alicia—the girl you want to call" since the girl in question was the one who'd entered herself in his contacts that way. It was accompanied by a photo of her dark-skinned, beautiful face. He gritted his teeth and hit "call."

Fucking women and graduating seemed like a decent new plan to him. She was at his place in ten minutes and they didn't leave the bed for twenty-four hours.

• • • •

BY THE TIME HE EARNED his degree from Vanderbilt Medical School and had gotten the matching placement emergency room residency back at Michigan, he'd worked his way through three-quarters of the women in his class, plus two professors, one of whom claimed she would lock him up in her basement if he tried to leave. So, status quo for his life, relationship-wise, he figured.

He was on his A-game, but for the clingy Alicia who'd spent one long afternoon crying at his table. She'd claimed she was pregnant, and that they had to get married. He'd gone out for a pregnancy test, which was negative—both of them, since she insisted on taking it twice. "Get out," he'd said, his head in his hands.

"Baby," she'd cooed, winding her arms around his neck from behind. He'd gripped them, pushed her away.

"No," he'd said. "I am an absolute shithead, Alicia. I've fucked everything with two legs and a pussy in the last six months, and I need to go home. Get the hell out of here. I'll be gone in ten days. You should go, have a life, find a nice guy. One that is not me."

"You're a shit. You'll never grow up. Screwing around with as many women as possible gets you nowhere, Craig, but maybe you don't care. Maybe you don't ever want to be happy."

He watched in silence as she grabbed all the various items of crap she'd left at his place over the last months. His ears buzzed and his heart ached. He wanted one thing—still. He picked up his phone and called Suzanne just after Alicia slammed the door.

"Hey," she said, making his chest release a bit of tension. "I got your email. So you're coming home?"

He sighed. "Yes. And I have something I want to ask you."

"Be careful Craig," she said, her slow, sexy voice making him get up and pace the room. "I don't want to hurt you. But I won't let you hurt me, either."

"Listen, Suzanne. I love you. And the last six months of bullshit have only convinced me of that even more. I'm afraid you're going to have to deal with it and even own up to your own feelings for a change."

She sighed. "Come home Craig. I'll be here."

"Two weeks," he said, leaning his head back and allowing relief to wash over him. "I'm moving back into my condo. "I miss you."

"I miss you too. See you soon."

Chapter Sixteen

"Hey, Red!" Suzanne's business partner Evan snapped his fingers under her nose. "We have a problem. Are you even listening?"

She shook her head, gulped some water, and tried to focus. The past four years that she'd known Craig Robinson had been so... strange. Something about him had struck her the moment she met him. His boyish, open manner, and extreme blond, casual good looks had her by the short hairs within minutes. That day—when he'd still been with Sara—was a life changer for her, and she knew it now. Admitting it to herself, however, was another thing altogether.

She brought her attention back to the crisis du jour at Big House Brewing. It was Summer Beer Fest week, and her entire staff had fallen victim to food poisoning they'd gotten at a pot luck staff picnic. Now, she and her business partner and whomever else they could convince to help them would handle everything at the giant beer fest.

Going back to the basics of pouring beer for thousands of drinkers at the largest two-day beer event in the Midwest sounded daunting, but something in her craved that kind of direct contact with her beer-drinking public.

"You and I have to set up and man the whole thing. I got it. I can get Craig." Evan raised an eyebrow at her, but she ignored him. "You bring Julie. Hell, see if Jack wants to help. God knows he knows as much about our beers as we do and he can run his fool mouth like a champ. We can do this."

She rose, feigning nonchalance, but her ears were fuzzy and her chest was tight. Craig was back today, at his old condo. He had something to ask her. Evan leaned back in his chair and studied her. "Craig, eh?"

"Yeah, what about him?" She stuck her laptop in her backpack and shuffled papers around, nervous, unsure, excited, something—all of it at once. Her hands shook, so she stopped and forced herself to calm. "Sorry. Didn't mean to snap at you."

"It's okay. You deserve some happiness, Suzanne. But do us all a favor and don't talk yourself out of it this time?"

Her face flamed hot, but she had no response. Her brief and intense relationship with Blake, Sara's brother, had ended badly for them both—but at her insistence. She'd spent plenty of hours second-guessing that choice, but based upon how happy Blake seemed now with her old college friend, Rob, and their brew pub, he'd ended up better off.

She hadn't had any sort of close, personal—much less physical—relationship since. But being alone didn't intimidate her. After surviving a marriage that had turned abusive and almost killed her, and then diving into a passionate affair with Blake, she convinced herself the time alone was required.

Since her last messy encounter with Craig in Nashville, she'd gone on a date with a man who had seemed promising. Marcus was a banker who'd moved from the west coast and hence had zero knowledge relative to her own convoluted past. He was a stable, good looking, successful older man and always hung out at the Tap Room on nights she was there. But the raw, physical connection she'd shared with Craig after they'd gotten to know each other as friends through the Jack and Sara drama had morphed into something much deeper for her. Something she'd been running from ever since.

But now, she needed to get a grip, as Evan reminded her. Not toss this amazing man away. If she could manage it.

She drove downtown, hoping to catch him at his place and break the news about the weekend that had devolved into a long one of schlepping equipment, kegs and other crap and two days of beer pouring. She'd spent way too much time in denial about him. She could admit that to herself now. Her continuous excuses about their age difference, her own emotional baggage, were all sounding pretty lifeless, especially to her.

The fact that they'd spent the last six months ignoring each other more or less, after that surprise visit she'd paid him, had been brutal for her. When she'd gotten the email telling her he'd matched at U of M for his ER residency, she'd burst into tears.

Her heart pounded all the way from the elevator to his place. The door was unlocked so she tiptoed in. The place was a mess of boxes, furniture, his various guitars and computers.

No Craig.

When she saw the one open box labeled "swim stuff" she smiled. She got back in the lift and went up to the top floor. The chlorine odor hit her hard and made her gasp with memory. Craig. Her brain and body both clamored for him.

She eased into the steamy room, her eyes unable to make out much, but her ears in tune to the soft splashes as he moved through the water. She took off her shoes and sat on one of the lounge chairs and watched the subtle play of his lean body cutting through the water, then flipping at the side and pushing off, emerging with his arms slicing through the blue.

You love him, Suzanne. He's an amazing man. Don't ruin this with your bullshit. You deserve this. So does he.

But a small, niggling, familiar voice of worry crept into her brain.

He'll want a family. You don't even know if you're capable of that.

She shook her head, ordering the voice quietly and kept watching him—the man who'd befriended her, made her laugh, made her sing with pleasure, and was back in her life once again.

After almost thirty minutes of nonstop crawl, then breaststroke, he stopped, hanging on to the edge of the pool with one hand. He wiped his face, took off his goggles, and the look of joy on his face when he saw her made her want to weep. But she stood, holding out a Big House Brewing tee shirt.

"Suit up hot stuff. We have work to do."

• • • •

IT WAS BRUTALLY HOT at the festival, as usual. Something like a hundred and six degrees in the shade, but that didn't stop the masses of beer fans. After a few mishaps getting the draft systems set up, Suzanne, Craig, Evan, and Julie were pouring, talking, and passing out temporary tattoos with the distinctive Big House logo to the thousands who descended on the event.

Jack would be along later, he claimed, after he dropped Katie off at Sara's. It was the little girl's birthday tomorrow and Craig would go to the party. Suzanne was determined not to let that bug her. The potential connection to Sara Thornton was one thing that hovered around Craig, like a sort of low-level haze, and she needed him to shake it off.

Now that he was back, he'd get pulled back into that life with the little girl who could be his biological daughter. It bugged her. Kind of a lot. But she was determined to talk to him about it.

She stopped at one point, heard a low rumble of thunder, and wiped the sweat from her face. Craig had taken over the temp tattoo station and was flirting his adorable ass off with every young woman who presented her chest, or hip, or face to him so he could press one of the damn things to her skin with a wet sponge.

He looked over at her and winked. She rolled her eyes and resumed the pour-talk-pour-talk that was the chief work of any beer fest. Lightning flickered through the tent, making the crowd gasp. The loud clap of thunder that followed made her jump, and as festival goers crowded into the three tents, it got darker and darker.

The rain, when it came, was a deluge as if the very heavens were pouring buckets straight onto them. She looked down at one point and discovered she was standing in four inches of water.

"Here." Craig handed her a sample cup of beer. "Might as well drink." He downed his and refilled it.

Rain pounded on the tent and continued to swirl around their ankles. The crowd got ever more raucous as the beer, heat and emotion she'd been suppressing for so long made her dizzy. Thunder and lightning headed east, but the rain remained a steady downpour. She stared at it, took another drink, and set the cup down. She grabbed Craig's hand. "C'mon." She tugged him away from the festival bar. "Let's cool off."

He tossed the temporary tattoos down and ran out with her. She splashed through puddles and mud, waved at all the various brewers and brewery owners calling out to her as she and Craig ran like crazy people towards the river that bordered the edge of the park. Her heart pounded in her ears, but she was honest-to-god happy for what seemed like the first time in years.

She pulled her hand out of his and stood, lifting her face to the cool rain. Then looked down to find him staring at her, breathing heavy, the grey brewery shirt molded to his amazing torso. "You look like a centerfold," she yelled out to him over the various noises.

"You should get a load of yourself." He nodded to her, laughing. She looked down. Her own thin tee and bra were soaked, and there was no disguising the hard peaks of her nipples. She looked over and saw ten or twelve of her colleagues huddled under a tent and giving her thumbs ups. She flushed red, and then looked at Craig, his long blond hair dripping and his dark brown eyes glistening.

"I missed you," she whispered, and before she could say another word, he had her scooped up and tossed over his shoulder to the hooting and loud applause of the nearby tent.

He jogged along the Huron River shore, taking them some distance from the crowds. Then he put her down and laid a kiss on her that made tears spring to her eyes. She leaned back against an ancient oak tree, pulling him with her. The rain kept up and got even harder, but she didn't care. His lips, his hands and body pressed to hers- that was what she felt, what she needed to be whole. He broke the kiss. She hooked her fingers in his belt loops and kept him close. "Kiss me like that some more."

"I will, don't worry. But first, my question." He propped his hands on either side of her and stared deep into her soul. "Will you marry me?"

She gulped. Her entire body tingled with something she identified as fear. "I can't... I mean, let's just.... Damn." She looked away. He stood back up, glaring at her. The rain slowed to a drizzle. She grabbed his arms. "We have too much to sort out—we can't jump into marriage. Not yet."

"No one is jumping into anything. I want this and so do you. Why wait? What's the point of that?"

"You still have feelings for Sara," she blurted out, and then slapped her hand over her mouth.

He ran a hand through his dripping hair and took a step back from her. She grabbed him again, kissed him with an urgency born of desperation. "It's okay," she said, muttering into his rough jaw. "You just need to get past it. Then we'll talk more. Until you do, it won't work. You'll always be wondering 'what if' about her. She and Jack can't seem to get their damn act together. She's alone with Katie. And you—you could well be that girl's father."

He tried to escape her grip, but she held on and felt the anguish rise in her throat, choking her. She kept whispering in his ear. "Decide how you feel about Sara now that you're back, and then come to me. I'll be here." She kissed him and ran as fast as she could, splashing back through the puddles and mud, skidding to a stop behind her own bar again.

She didn't see him again for almost a month. By then she'd worked up the courage to tell him everything, how she got the scars, about

Blake, all of it. Then he could run away if he wanted. But at least he would know everything.

Chapter Seventeen

Their lives led them on different paths. Craig's killer schedule as an intern at the busy University of Michigan Emergency Room led to stress that settled right between her eyes and would not let go. She'd done this. This forced retreat was of her own design and she knew it, but she also knew it was true. He had to get past whatever residual shit he had with Sara.

In the month after the beer fest, they talked a few times on the phone, exchanged some texts, and saw each other once. The exhaustion and anxiety in his eyes while he sat and drank a few beers at her bar made her heart ache.

She was doing it again. Throwing away a perfectly good man thanks to her own... what? Inferiority complex? Inability to commit? She slumped down in the chair after he'd given her a noncommittal brush of lips and left, claiming he had early rounds in the morning.

The day after that encounter, her phone buzzed as she worked her way through some inventory problems. She frowned at it—why in the world would Sara be calling?

"Hi Suzanne." The woman's voice was firm and clear. "I wanted to invite you and Craig up to the lake house this weekend."

"Oh, um, well..." She hesitated.

"He said he has three days off and I wanted us to get together, all of us. Away from Ann Arbor."

"I don't know...."

"Listen, you realize better than anyone how I feel about Jack. Anything with Craig was—is—over. He's a friend. But I want him to be happy."

She closed her eyes, let her brain visit the fact that it just might work. "I'll talk to him. Thanks for the invite and for telling me that. It means a lot."

"I can't imagine two people who deserve happiness more. Take it from me—delaying that will only lead to disaster."

She hung up and sent him a text. "So about this lake weekend? You were going to mention that to me at some point?"

He responded within seconds. "Yes. But I need to go there by myself."

Her heart sank as she typed. "Ok."

His reply was fast again. "It's time for me to let her go, like you said. And I will, but want to talk to her first."

· · · ·

CRAIG STOOD, HIS HEART pounding, staring at Sara. They'd walked along the Lake Michigan shoreline together and he'd been about half-convinced that Suzanne had been right. He did harbor lingering feelings for her. They'd been through a lot, after all. And he might be Katie's father.

He'd been about two seconds from kissing her, but she'd stopped him, and he was grateful for that. "Go to her," Sara told him. He nodded, turned, and sprinted up the beach, taking the steps up to the house two at a time, not even hesitating at the concept of another three-hour trip back to Ann Arbor.

The lake house was in chaos when he hit the door. Katie, the seven-year-old mini-Sara, was screaming her head off. Blake was trying to stop the blood that seemed to be coming from her foot.

Craig picked her up, used his best doctor voice to calm her as he took the wet rag Blake held out to press to her foot. "I need to look at it honey, okay, so hang onto Uncle Blake's hand for a second." She hiccupped, nodded, and did as he said while he pulled the sharp stick out of her instep. She flinched but didn't cry, instead heaving a sigh when he smeared antibiotic cream on the wound and bound it with gauze and tape.

As he held her on his lap, he acknowledged how much he loved holding her small, warm body. The natural caretaker in him tightened his grip on her as she resumed her hitching sobs. This could be his daughter. He shut his eyes at the force of it.

"Uncle Craig," the girl whispered. "I missed you. I'm glad you're back."

He looked up and saw Blake. But instead of giving him his usual positive energy sort of look, he was frowning. He knelt down beside them. He stroked her hair. She vacated Craig's lap and launched herself at Blake.

"What happened? Who was on the phone before you ran outside and hurt your foot?" he asked them both.

"Uncle Jack..." Katie sucked in a hitching breath and buried her face in Blake's neck. "He's not coming. I wanted to see him and he's not coming out here like he promised."

Rob grabbed a phone and started dialing. Craig looked up, puzzled. "Hey," Rob spoke into the phone. Blake and Craig both listened to one side of a difficult sounding conversation. When he hung up, his face was pale. "It's Maureen, Jack's sister," he said to Craig. "Well, actually it's her husband, Brandis. He's, uh, he's dead."

"Shit," Blake muttered and walked out to the deck after handing Katie off to Rob. Craig stood. This whole thing had gotten surreal, but his need to get back to Suzanne was suffocating him. He walked out and stood by Blake. "Why are you even here?" the man asked, keeping his eyes trained down on the deck.

Craig frowned. Blake had always been in his corner when it came to Sara. The guy turned to him, his deep green eyes resigned. "I mean, why are you not with Suzanne?"

Craig heaved a sigh. The ghostly memory of Katie in his arms, the almost-moment he'd shared with Sara all roiled around his head. But something else was stronger now—the vision of a petite, beautiful red head he wanted to hold in his arms more than he wanted to drink water.

Blake put a hand on his arm. "Go. I've got this." He nodded back to the small lake house where they could still hear Katie snuffling her way through little-girl disappointment. Craig felt a shit-eating grin spread over his face. "Jesus, go already. What are you waiting for, an engraved invitation?" Blake waved him away.

The wind whipped his face as he sped back the way he had just come, going east now, towards Ann Arbor. His heart was light, his body on fire, and he had one thing in mind.

Going to Suzanne, being with her, and nothing else. The walk with Sara, the moment with Katie, then Blake's sudden understanding of how it should be between them all, it all pointed to one thing—he and Sara were well, and truly, over. And now he had to prove it to Suzanne.

He screeched up outside her house, put his helmet on the seat, and then saw her glowing like a beacon in a yellow sundress. "About time," she said as he bounded up the steps, collecting her in his arms and diving right into her, unwilling to ever come up for air again.

• • • •

HE SAT, GASPING FOR breath, his brain refusing to process what she was saying. Their bodies had connected, and Craig had never been happier even though it was immediate, quick and right on her front porch. Until words like "rape," and "glass" and "steps" and "dead" rolled through him, as she recounted the complete story of what had happened between her and Mitchell Baxter.

Blake had come along at the wrong and the right time for her, and after Mitchell had delivered his final, brutal beating to the small, shivering woman he held in his arms, the young man had landed that asshole in the hospital.

Craig clenched his fists, rose and paced, stared out into the dark. Her voice broke, but she kept talking. His jaw ached. He forced himself to stop gritting his teeth. She pulled her legs up close, held onto herself as the story unfolded.

Mitchell, home from his stint in the hospital a few days after her. Suzanne, on this very porch waiting for him, and realizing that she had to do something or he would without a doubt kill her the next time. His angry voice, clattering up the steps, then with a simple push the man fell back, his broken leg giving him no purchase. And the distinct sound of a broken skull on the large granite step.

He shut his eyes. "Stop," he croaked out, unable to take more.

"No," she said, her voice strong. "I need you to hear it all."

He took the few steps between them and scooped her up, held her close and kept listening. Blake's insistence on staying with her, her first time having sex after Mitchell's brutality with his body and broken glass. All of it, she spared him no detail. He kissed her hair, rubbed her back as she started shivering. She put her head on his shoulder. "I'm a real mess. You sure you want any part of this?"

"Go on," he whispered. "How did it end?"

She wiped her arm across her face. "I made him go. I... I loved him, like I told you. But he was too much a part of the worst part of my life. I needed to get myself back on track and every time I saw him, I saw Mitchell... could hear the glass, and me screaming, smell blood. It was so unfair to Blake. I'm still coming to terms with it."

"He seems to have landed on his feet, with Rob." Craig brushed her hair off her face.

She sighed and relaxed. "Yes. Thank god. I'm so happy for them. Although it's beyond weird too, all the connections. I mean, Rob was one of my best friends in college. And the whole Jack and Sara thing... Jesus."

Craig held her close. "I'm grateful for Blake," he said.

She looked away from him, but he turned her chin and made her face him. "He saved your life." He brushed a kiss over her trembling lips. "And I'm grateful for Sara. She introduced us, remember?"

She nodded and put her arms around his neck, giving him a much more meaningful kiss. He stood and carried her inside. "Now, let me set about proving to you how grateful I am, you sexy ginger girl you."

Chapter Eighteen

Craig rolled over, draping an arm across Suzanne's hip. She shifted, mumbled and molded against him, bringing every part of him awake. The sun pierced the blinds, hitting him square in the eye; he buried his face in her neck, killing a couple of birds with one stone. He let his hand trail along her hip, down one leg, then up, reveling in the way she sighed and turned to face him.

"Mmm..." he muttered into her ear, realizing he'd almost missed the night, the opportunity—hell, had almost missed her. His heart raced, but then calmed when she touched him. He closed his eyes, leaned into the cool palm she put against his face.

"I'm glad you came back." Her voice tickled his ear as she snuggled in, tucking herself into the curve of his body.

"Me too, especially if you keep doing that." She trailed her hand across his shoulder, down to his bare hip, then forward to grip his morning-hard cock. "Yeah. That."

She giggled into his chest and kept moving her hand up and down, both torturing and pleasuring when she would stop and use his own fluid to lubricate her action. His hips thrust, matching her movements. The sensation of her lips and teeth against his nipple made him moan, but he bit it back, tried to resist, wanting to please her first.

"Let it go Craig," she whispered, as her lips made their way up his neck. Her firm breasts pressed against him and her hand kept that amazing activity on his flesh. "Come for me," she demanded as she licked her way back down and captured his nipple between her teeth once more.

"Shit," he grunted and allowed himself the intense pleasure of release. He leaned his head back as the orgasm gathered strength at the base of his spine, then roared up and captured his brain, making him cry out. He held her close as his body kept zinging while spasms of pleasure thrummed through every nerve ending.

"Good morning." She tilted her face up and kissed him, thrusting her tongue into his mouth, making something wild rise in him, something he couldn't name and didn't understand. He held her close as they kissed, then flipped her over, holding her arms down as he did his own tongue dance down her neck, to her breasts. He sucked first one, then the other luscious nipple before sinking down between her legs and tasting every glorious centimeter of her sex.

She groaned and gripped his hair, wrapped both legs around him, and tilted her hips up, meeting him halfway. He flicked at the hard nub of her clit, teased around it as he slid a finger inside the tight glove of her body. "Stop that," she said, making him smile before he tugged her clit between his lips, sucking hard. Her body clenched. He relished the approach of her orgasm with all of his senses.

"Oh yes!" Her hiss of satisfaction filled his ears, and he groaned when his cock shifted and hardened again. He gripped her hips and held her body close, needing a different sort of connection. Needing it so badly he might explode if he couldn't get inside her within the next few seconds.

She gasped as he climbed up between her legs. "What?" Her eyes were bright, her grin infectious.

"Oh nothing." He tried to calm his own breathing, but the sensation of her legs around his waist and the heat of her pussy against his aching shaft made him breathless. "Just thought we might...."

"What?" She angled her hips, and he sighed as he slipped inside her, loving the grip of her body. "What did you think we might do?" She threaded her fingers through his hair and tugged him close to her lips. She thrust against him, using her inner muscles to grip him hard. "This is what I think you might like."

"Good call." Craig pulled out, then thrust in, just to experience that amazing stretch and give of her body around his. He stared at her as their bodies connected, each of them moving in a perfect rhythm. "I figured you for a pretty smart girl. Guess I was right."

"Harder," she whispered, running her hands down his face, across his shoulders, and down his chest. Every inch of his skin tingled; every nerve ending was on fire. The urge to possess her, to prove something, to be everything she would ever need, made him close his eyes against the powerful desire to say the words she wasn't ready to hear.

Not yet. Not after the hard truths he'd laid on him last night. He still reeled from it and his brain buzzed with fury at her dead asshole of a husband and with sympathy for Blake.

She reached back, gripped the headboard, and lifted her hips high. His brain fogged. His cock jerked and his lips betrayed him at the last minute in that split second after a knee-melting orgasm, which turns a man into a quivering pile of useless flesh. Her body bucked against his, the pulse and contraction of her climax pulling him even further into the deep recesses of words he wanted to say but shouldn't.

He collapsed down onto her, their sweat slicking their flesh. "I love you, Suzanne." She started to stiffen beneath him, but Craig lifted his face from her breasts and held her still. "You might as well accept that."

He collapsed down beside her and tugged her close, kissing her lips, her cheeks, her hair. "Okay," she muttered into his chest. "But you might regret it."

"I doubt that very much." He relaxed as sleep stole across his orgasm-addled brain.

When he woke to the irritating loop of banjo music from his phone, she was gone. He squinted at the phone's screen, groaned, then showered, found an apple in the kitchen and saw her sitting out on the patio cradling a steaming cup of coffee to her chest. After watching her a minute, he left her alone, figuring that was best. He scribbled out a note and left it propped on the coffee maker, filled a travel mug, and left.

"See you tomorrow. But I'll be in touch before that. Love, C"

Suzanne heard him moving around in the kitchen and got that weird split sensation in her chest again. She knew damn good and well how he felt about her. Craig had fallen into her life at such a strange moment for them both. But as much as she wanted him, wanted to be with him forever, another darker something kept reminding her it should not be. The physical scars had healed, but she wondered if the emotional ones would ever fade. She sipped, staring out into the woods at the edge of the yard.

Mitchell, her late husband, had loved her at one time. Then he let obsession get the best of him, which had turned into a frightening abuser. He had almost killed her, too, that last time, here in this house. She shut her eyes, forced it out and tried to recall Craig's words, his arms, lips and hands.

Her phone buzzed at her elbow, but she ignored it in favor of reliving the many romantic moments she'd shared with Craig. Forcing memories of Mitchell's angry face out of her head.

Her face flushed, recalling last night when he'd roared up on that stupid motorcycle and declared he loved her, even after she told him her horrible story. She sighed, stretched out her well-sated body and thought back to the moment she'd met him, when Sara had introduced them at the Big House Tap Room. She'd berated herself about the sudden attraction.

For Christ's sake, what was it with you and younger men?

She shook her head, finished the coffee, and stood.

The phone kept buzzing. She glanced at it and saw Rob had been calling her for the last fifteen minutes. Hitting redial as she wandered back inside, she made a mental note to call Jack and get this house listed and sold.

The damn place echoed with the ghosts of her former life—the sounds of her angry, abusive spouse, her own screams of fear and their loud arguments. Then the shattering of glass that last night, when he'd raped her, beaten her and cut her so badly she had to have multiple plastic surgeries for her face. And she still hadn't owned up to the facts of the damage he did to her baby-making anatomy. Doctors warned her about her ability to have kids. But she never had it confirmed. It seemed like too much to take on, and besides, until now, who cared? She took it at face value, and her irregular cycle didn't help matters any.

The thought of her comfortable little downtown condo—the place where she'd retreated after breaking it off with Blake—made her smile as her friend answered the phone.

"Suze, have you heard from Jack?"

She poured more coffee, still only half listening, as the Craig-fixated part of her brain warmed her from the inside out. "No. Why?"

"He's on his way to Germany."

She stopped stock still, unsure if she heard him correctly.

"Yeah," Rob went on. "It's Maureen's husband, Brandis. He's dead."

"Oh God," She sank into a kitchen chair, her hands shaking. Jack's brother-in-law had been one of his best friends from high school and had married Jack's sister when they'd been very young. Brandis and Maureen had twins, a boy and a girl, and were about to move back to the states after seven years overseas.

"Anyway, I wanted you to know."

"Okay, thanks." She clicked off. Then hit Jack's speed dial, thinking to at least leave him a message of support. Jack had been her first crush in college, but after one hot connection they agreed to stay friends. And he'd been steadfast for her for years since.

"Hey." His voice sounded close.

"Hey yourself." She leaned back in the chair and tried to think about what she could say at this point. "I'm sorry, honey. So very sorry."

"Yeah, it's, um, a real mess."

"You're there already?"

Jack heaved a sigh. "Airport. Waiting for a cab."

"Well, I'm around if you want to talk about it."

"I heard you turned down a perfectly legit proposal."

The sudden change of subject made her frown. Then she realized what he was talking about and the frown deepened. "None of your business. Shit, news travels fast in our circle."

"Someday you're going to let go of that chokehold you have on yourself. The one that makes you think you aren't allowed to be happy."

"You concentrate on helping your family over there. Let me worry about my happiness."

"Okay, okay I hear you. But, please realize that a lot of us think you deserve to cut yourself some slack. You sliced Blake out of your life and that worked out fine for him, but...."

"All right, spare me, Gordon. He's..." She stopped, unsure what she could say about Craig. She realized she missed him already. And then, in the same thought, acknowledged she would continue to push him away.

Jack broke the silence. "I know, honey. He's a great guy. If anybody knows that, I do."

She smiled. "Go on, do what you gotta do. Call me later if you need anything. I'll check in with Sara too, and Katie."

"Thanks babe. You're the best."

"And to think you took a pass...."

He chuckled. "Oh, I would have just fucked your life up even more. I'll call you later. Bye."

She sat and stared at her phone for a long time, contemplating the many odd turns her life had indeed taken to lead her here.

Chapter Nineteen

Craig lay back on the blanket under the huge tree, loving the sensation of Suzanne's head resting on his leg as she propped there, holding her e-reader. It was one of his rare days off and they'd had a picnic by the river. His stomach was full. His heart stuffed with unsaid words.

He ran his fingers through her hair, loving the silky feel of it, unwilling to ruin the moment by talking. She valued her silences, and he was getting used to them, coming to appreciate them even. The sun moved towards the horizon, sending long shadows between the trees around the edge of the river.

The high-pitched squeal of kids made him sit up. A couple of families were engaged in an impromptu soccer game, the parents encouraging what looked to be five-year-olds to kick the ball past their friends and into a small net. He smiled at the scene.

The unmistakable sensation of Suzanne's mood change as she moved away from him made him wish he hadn't paid any attention. He put a hand on her knee. Her thousand-yard stare remained fixed in place. He cursed himself, cursed the innocent families. "Listen, Suzanne, you can't always get all twitchy when there are kids around. I don't give two shits about...."

She stood, brushing off her jeans, ending further conversation. Anger pierced him, pushing his usual laid-back attitude under a layer of frustration that was becoming entirely too familiar. He grabbed her hand. "Don't walk away from me."

She glared at him, tension oozing out of every pore. "Why not?"

"God, but you are the most obtuse woman on the planet. Sit down."

She raised an eyebrow, settled that familiar "I don't give a shit" look on her face and sat. He swallowed hard.

"Listen, I realize that I rushed you early on. I 'm glad you thought we should get to know each other. I needed to purge Sara out of my system, to understand my feelings for you. I did both of those things. So I don't get what more I can do to prove to you how I feel."

She blew out a breath, bent her knees and wrapped her arms around them as if trying to draw in on herself even further. It took all he had not to wrap his arms around her and soothe her out of her funk, but he kept his distance and looked into her eyes. "Talk to me, Suzanne. I can't take much more of this."

"Much more of what?" She looked away. "We're having fun, aren't we? You get laid on a regular basis."

Craig's heart pounded as his temper rose. He kept his mouth shut, though. She let the silence spin out for a few minutes before speaking, and her word sent a sharp pain through his gut.

"I warned you Craig. I'm damaged. I can't be what anyone needs me to be, other than maybe a girlfriend and beer marketing expert. Don't pressure me."

"I'm not pressuring you. But I'll be damned if every time you think I am looking at a kid, or a family, you flip out on me."

"I'm not flipping out."

"You did not three minutes ago."

She looked straight at him. The hurt in her eyes made him grind his teeth with anger. If that asshole of an abusive husband were alive at that moment, he would gladly kill him all over again. He gripped her hands.

"I love you Suzanne. I won't ever stop, but I'm starting to get the feeling that you'll never allow yourself to be loved."

She yanked her hands out of his at the same moment his phone clanged with an emergency call. He cursed, grabbed it, and answered. His heart nearly skipped a beat when he heard the nurse's words and the distinct sound of his friend Sara crying hysterically in the background.

Suzanne bit back tears, ugly words, rejection, anything she could. Grateful the phone had interrupted them before she really ruined everything in a knee-jerk, ill-considered retort. She watched as he walked away. Admired the strong line of his shoulders, his long, lean legs, his shaggy, boyish blond hair. She clenched her fists.

Get a grip, Suzanne. Why won't you let him...

She looked up when he yelled her name.

"Let's go." He grabbed the picnic basket and held out a hand to help her to her feet.

"What is it?" The look in his eyes was wild.

"It's Katie. She's in my ED."

Suzanne's heart sped up, and she followed him up the hill to the car. She loved the little girl, too. It was impossible not to. She knew damn good and well that the child was Jack's daughter—she had to be. Only that man's gene pool would create a small human who was adored by everyone who met her, but whose hair trigger temper could get the best of her.

Craig sped down the hill towards the U of M emergency department, jumped out, and tossed the keys to her. She whispered that she loved him as he ran inside, only to discover that Katie's appendix had burst and she needed emergency surgery to save her life.

The players all emerged one by one. Jack appeared in a tux, trailing the woman he'd been seeing since he and Sara were on the outs. Sara was there already pacing the hall. The two of them exchanged words Suzanne couldn't hear but, based on their body language and faces she presumed were harsh.

Jack looked startled when Craig spoke before grabbing the computer tablet he was holding and signing something on the screen after Sara dropped into a chair, sobbing. Jack disappeared then returned after about twenty minutes, rolling his shirtsleeve down.

Rob showed up next and put an arm around Sara, instantly calming her. Blake ran out of the elevator, his eyes wild with worry. Suzanne smiled, watching him huddle with his sister.

Blake had been crucial in her life once. A catalyst and a healing force, and one she'd pushed away for reasons she sometimes still doubted. But he had found happiness. That much was clear. Rob crouched behind the two of them, calming everyone as always he managed to do.

At one point, she sensed a hand on her shoulder and realized she must have dozed off in one of the hard waiting room chairs. Rob smiled at her and dropped into a nearby seat.

"Hey." She snuggled into the arm he put around her. The man was truly incredible. He had provided such a balm for Blake, Sara—for everyone, really. When she, Jack and Rob, had met in college all those years ago, she'd somehow known Rob would be the rock for them all. Thank god his cancer seemed to be in remission.

"How's it going, Red?" He kissed her temple. They sat and watched Sara, Blake, and Jack, sitting vigil.

Craig appeared in the doorway, still wearing his day-off outfit of jeans and a soft oxford button-down shirt. They all stood, but Suzanne and Rob stayed back, let him talk with them first. Jack's sister showed up, her deep blue gaze frantic until she laid eyes on her brother. When he stomped out of the room, after getting the update from Craig, she followed him. Suzanne's head started to ache.

Craig leaned against the wall, eyes closed. Suzanne rose and went to him, putting a hand on his shoulder. She gasped when he clutched at her, but realized he was trying to hold it together for the sake of Katie's mother. He pulled her out of the room, held her close.

"She's going to be okay. But holy hell, Suzanne, the surgeon told me she coded on the table. Twice. Jesus."

She stayed quiet, letting him get it out of his system. Her heart clenched at his next words.

"Well, one mystery is solved. She is definitely Jack's. I ran the match on her blood type. He was the only possible donor."

Suzanne smiled at him, placing a hand on his stubbled cheek. "I'm sorry." She swallowed the lump building in her throat at the convoluted daytime-drama nature of their situation.

He grabbed her hand, kissed it, and looked deep into her eyes. "I'm not." He leaned into her ear. "Thanks for staying around."

"Of course." Her eyes burned with unshed tears. Words choked her, but she forced them up and out. "I can't ever be that for you. We won't ever be parents. I can't...." Her voice broke, the residual stress making her shake so hard her teeth rattled.

He cradled her face between his hands, brushed his lips over hers. "How many times do I have to tell you?"

The sound of Jack barreling back through the double doors cut him off. Her old friend shot her a look of utter agony.

The past few years had been so stressful for him. He'd lost his father, one of his best friends and brother-in-law, and lived through the whole situation with Sara. Why the two of them wouldn't or couldn't get it together, it boggled the mind. Perhaps they were too much alike. Because they were. Apparently, fatally so. She wondered if somehow it could work out for them now with the simple reality of confirmed parenthood.

Craig led Jack over to the ICU window, muttering words of encouragement, and opened the door. Suzanne swallowed hard, walked over to Sara, and pulled her away from her brother.

"It's okay. She's fine. You guys are going to be fine. But seriously, Sara, you need to go to Jack. He needs you. I know what a tough asshole the guy can be, but I swear to God he loves you. Please let him."

Sara looked at her with something resembling relief in her eyes, pushed the door open, and walked to Katie's bedside. When she laid her hand on Jack's shaking shoulder, he jumped to his feet, knocking over his chair, and grabbed onto her, his face a mask of relief. Suzanne turned and left, unable to cope with it any longer.

Chapter Twenty-Two

The sun was at that perfect moment, nearly an hour before setting along the edge of Lake Michigan. Craig squinted behind his sunglasses, gripping Suzanne's hand tight as they watched Jack and Sara finally tie the knot. Their words were soft, heartfelt, the whole scene flawless. When he looked over at Rob, the doctor in him saw the pallor, heard the rattle in his chest. It was so not fair to anyone here. But the guy was declining again and fast.

Suzanne put her arm around his waist. Her new willingness to be affectionate with him in public was such a relief. They still hadn't finished the conversation about family, but things had been good, or at least minus too much drama as Katie recovered. Sara had met him at the door a few weeks ago when he and Suzanne were going to take the stir-crazy girl to the Detroit zoo for the day. He'd taken one look at her and known.

"Hey, does Jack know you're pregnant again?"

She'd blushed, put a hand on her still flat stomach. "Jesus, what are you, psychic? I only did the test this morning."

"Nah, I can tell, I guess. Congrats. Hopefully, this time will be less stressful for you both."

She'd given him a fierce hug and held on to his arms. "How is it with you guys? Really?"

"It's fine. She's moved out of that mansion now that Jack has it on the market." He'd run a hand down his face, frustration at her reluctance to commit making him angry. "Anyway, as long as I don't make her plan beyond next weekend, we're okay. I guess."

Sara had patted his shoulder. "She's been through a lot."

He had shrugged her off. "I know."

Suzanne had agreed to accompany him to Jack and Sara's lakeside wedding, which is sisters-in-law all claimed was "a milestone date."

He'd booked a room at a cozy, romantic bed-and-breakfast and planned to make it a weekend she would never forget. He leaned down, sucked in a breath. The spicy, cinnamon essence of her filled his nose, making his body come to attention in a fairly embarrassing show.

"You okay?" He ran his hand down her hip, across her ass.

She pressed closer to him. "I'm gonna be better soon, I think." She bit his ear as the crowd burst into applause at the sight of Jack and Sara's kiss.

"Yes, you will be." He willed himself down from a lusty ledge and clapped along with the rest of the crowd.

The photographer posed people in loose, casual groups. He sat with Suzanne and Katie for one of the pictures, all of them wearing cool looks and Ray Bans, draped around lounge chairs. He chatted with Rob, tried to resist the urge to pull the guy inside for some rest as he looked positively haggard.

He had a couple of beers, but kept a close eye on her—his woman, darting in and around, doing her usual thing, comfortable in a crowd. At one point, he saw Sara take a seat as Jack handed her a glass of lemonade. Lila, the woman Rob and Blake had chosen as their surrogate, pulled a chair up to her. The two women spoke and hugged. Jack shook Rob's, then Blake's hand.

Craig and Suzanne had discussed that whole thing and wondered how objective the relationship was—how much of it was contractual and how much emotional. Suzanne suspected that Blake had fallen in love with the woman and Craig hoped they could sustain the relationship as Rob's disease kept progressing.

He smiled. Baby mission accomplished, he surmised, and none too soon, if Rob was going to be around to see the child born. He shook his head at the evil twist of fate for his friends. He smiled when he felt arms around his waist. He pulled Suzanne around to his side, kissed her and hoped like hell she didn't get upset.

"Good news?" She nodded in the direction of the people still gathered around the two women.

He tensed. "Yeah. I guess. Hey, how long do we have to stay here? I have a schedule."

She raised an eyebrow at him, then rose up on tiptoes to kiss his cheek. "Thanks," she said.

"You're welcome. For what I don't know, I'm sure, unless you're thanking me in advance of how hard I'm gonna rock you this weekend."

She blushed, and the sight of that made him want to pick her up, toss her over his shoulder, and get the hell out of here. "Well, okay. But thanks for something else."

"For what, my lovely, blushing, ginger girl?"

"For not rushing me. I mean, after that first time."

He sighed and held her closer. They watched Katie and her friend, Lila's daughter Maddie, run around in their fancy dresses as the sun set. Blake was out lighting several small bonfires. The party ramped up as people drank more. They found an empty lounge chair and sat together. She leaned back into him and kept his hands on both her arms, his lips to her ear.

Jack and Sara stood apart for a while, deep in conversation. The smile on Sara's face made Craig happy for her and even for Jack.

"Let's go," he whispered. "I'm horny."

She elbowed him, but giggled when he tugged her up, slid his hand up her skirt, and pulled her into a shadow of the deck. "Oooh, naughty." She met his lips, let him dive into her mouth with his tongue as he slid a finger along her lacey excuse for panties.

"Careful, I'm liable to jump you here. And we have such a nice room waiting." He lingered over her lips for a moment.

She looked away, and Craig had a second of panic. Her emotional volatility had evened out in the last months, thank God. But he was not about to entertain any of that nonsense this weekend. It was one of the few times he was totally off the clock, had an entire three days to himself. He planned to spend it making Suzanne as happy as he could. For the entire fucking time.

Suzanne had a mild buzz by the time they made their stumbling way down the Lake Michigan beach and to the small B&B Craig had reserved for them. The whole day had been on the surreal side, with all the many convoluted connections between the wedding party and guests. She'd been thrilled to see her friend Jack happy—finally. She hoped the two of them could see their way clear to make it really work. The romantic sundown wedding was truly only the beginning of a long road to marital happiness.

"Hey!" she yelped when Craig picked her up and tossed her over his shoulder for the last few feet up the steps to the front porch. She slid down his strong, lean body, sucked in a breath of the ever-present chlorine smell. "Hey," she repeated in a whisper, fighting the urge to cry at the perfection of the moment. Here she was, happy, in the arms of the man she could picture sharing her life with—but still a bone-deep terror gripped her.

Craig put a finger under her chin and made her look at him. She gulped, smiled, and reached up to clutch his shaggy blond hair. His crooked smile filled her vision as he slanted his lips over hers, easygoing, tender, yet firm. The true essence of the man and everything she loved about him. His hands roamed up and down her back, gripped her ass, then moved up to twine in her hair. Her body heated up fast.

"I need....," she gasped, unsure how to put into words what it was she truly needed at that moment. Wishing more than anything that she could.

He reached behind her to open the door, and they kissed and groped their way down the dark hallway to their room. He grabbed her around the waist and tossed her onto the tall, creaky bed. Candles were already lit. A bottle of something sat chilling in a silver stand. She smiled at the sight of a bowl of Reese's Pieces sitting on the bedside table.

She giggled and moved her hips, making the bed moan and sing out a rusty sounding tune. Craig eyed her as he unzipped his khakis and yanked his already unbuttoned shirt off, dumping everything on the floor.

She put her hands behind her head, watching and marveling for the millionth time at his amazing body. His tall, lean strength was encased in a slender yet wiry build, with cut abs and broad swimmer's shoulders. A minimum of soft blond body hair led a nice trail straight to his sex, which at that moment was fully erect, its impressive length always a breathtaking sight.

"Lovely," she said as he put his hands on hips, keeping his distance. "What are you way over there for?" He smiled, and her heart pounded in her chest. "Craig... I...." She bit her lip.

He stayed put, not doing his usual jump in, undress and fuck her silly. He obviously wanted her to make the first move, but she was sure it wasn't something physical he wanted, despite his body's obvious need. Her throat closed up, but she forced herself to speak.

"This is very special. Thanks for arranging it."

The candles flickered from an invisible breeze in the slightly drafty room.

"No problem." He kept his voice low and his position across the room from her. "It's kind of a bizarre set of circumstances, but worth the getaway time."

"Yeah." She stood, slipped the straps of her sundress down, letting the soft silk pool at her feet. It had taken her a long time to come to terms with her own body, after what she'd been through. And she'd broken the heart of a very special man in the process. But it had brought her here, to this moment, with this equally special, but different man. And for that, she was wholly grateful.

She opened her mouth and let the words tumble out, keeping her inner self-editor in a strangle hold. "I love you, Craig. So much. So much I'm terrified. And I can't figure out why." Tears pressed behind her eyes, but she kept them at bay.

He stepped into her space, ran his hands up and down her freezing arms. She wrapped herself around him, loving the sensation of his warm skin, his sex pressed between them, his lips on her hair.

Craig's innate calm, the laid-back way he approached pretty much everything he did soothed her a lot more than those early days of frantic physicality with Blake. She knew his presence had helped her at that particular time in her life. But it had also hindered her ability to cope on her own. By burying herself away with Blake, ignoring the world and her part in it, she'd made it worse. So she'd ripped herself from him, hurting them both in the process.

But now... she sighed, kissed Craig's chest, worked her lips over to the erect pink bud of one nipple.

"Mmm hmm..." He threaded fingers in her hair as she lapped and nipped at his flesh. "Hang on." He tugged her over to the bed, opened the side table drawer and pulled out a small velvet box. She shut her eyes.

"Craig..."

But he put her hand to his lips, then kissed her there, and worked his way up the inside of her wrist, making her whole body break out in erotic tremors. He nipped the inside of her elbow. The light hit his dark eyes as she watched him kiss his way up to her shoulder. He pressed her back onto the bed, his hands cupping a breast, flicking a nipple.

"Open up," he whispered.

She closed her eyes, trusting him completely, and bit down on the crunchy peanut chocolate candy combination. He had a handful of them, and put them one by one on her chest, making a little trail down between her breasts to her stomach. She giggled when he dug one out of her navel, then gasped when he ran out of them, anticipating his talented lips on her sex.

But he raised his head, eyebrow cocked, and put another line of the stupid things up her body, reaching her lips and putting one, then another into her mouth. She sighed as he ran his hands over her now aching nipples, then teased her clit a half second, just long enough to make her whimper and lift her hips.

"Open your eyes, Suzanne." His voice was rough with repressed lust. She knew it when she heard it. She opened them, not even remembering when she closed them and saw it. The small, velvet box, now perched between her breasts in place of the candy.

She bit her lip, put her hands behind her head, and stared at him.

"So you're bribing me? Holding out until I answer this question?" She nodded to the jeweler's box.

"There's no question in there. Just a present."

She narrowed her eyes. She'd already turned down one proposal from him. Declared herself unwilling to even consider marrying again, no matter who asked. That had been several years ago and his willingness to stick it out, to stay with her, go at her pace, and at every turn, making her blissfully happy in mind and body had gone a long way.

"I can't."

"You can't what? Open a box?"

She shifted up so her back was against the headboard. Her whole body trembled as the word "yes" hovered against her lips. She opened it and smiled at the sight of a gorgeous emerald pendant, framed by two diamonds, all set in an art déco design of platinum. A tear dropped onto her leg. Damn the man.

She looked up and held it out. He fastened it around her neck and the beautiful gems settled onto her chest. "It's perfect," she whispered, touching it like a talisman. "You're perfect."

"Huh, about damn time you figured that out."

She grinned and grabbed his hand. "You're right. Now, bring that perfection over here mister and do what you will to me. Quick. Before I explode."

He grinned and crawled up between her legs, lapping at every inch of her skin, starting low and ending with her lips, shoving his tongue between them, sweeping inside at the exact moment he penetrated her with a long, luxurious stroke of his hips. She wrapped her legs around him, took him even deeper, her body stretching to accommodate him.

"Look at me, Suzanne," Craig whispered as he propped himself up. She put her hands to his face, ran her thumb across his lips, tilted her hips, making him blow out a breath and groan. "Good God, woman, you are enough to make a man lose control."

"Lose it, Craig. Don't hold back. Please." She cried out in pleasure when he shoved into her, pulled out, then thrust even deeper. "I... oh..." She arched up, tightened her grip.

His movements got faster, but he held her gaze. Then, at the last moment when her own release teetered on the horizon, threatening to bowl her over, he kissed her so hard the orgasm roared up from her core. And she finally realized all the fuss about "seeing fireworks." Her body pulsed, spasmed and clutched at him.

He tore his lips from hers. She put her hands on his face, loving the intensity of his release.

"I feel you inside me, Craig. I can feel you coming." A powerful vision flashed across her mind just then, making her heart stutter. Her body rolled through the climax, milking him, but her head ached as images of a child, a baby she would never be able to carry, made tears leak from her eyes.

"Holy hell." He sucked in deep breaths, leaned down to kiss her neck as his hips kept moving.

"That was...hey." He stopped, seeing the tears. "You okay? Did I hurt you?"

She shook her head, furious with herself for ruining an incredible moment and determined to salvage it.

"No, no, you know, girls. We cry at the strangest moments."

Later, after they'd shared the Imperial stout he'd been chilling and eaten more of the candies, he'd rolled over, tugged her close, curving his body around hers. But the clear as day images of a baby with a shock of blond hair and hazel eyes, looking up at her as she held it to her breast, made her breathless. She finally had to slip out of bed and sit in the chair to stop the sobs racking her body.

She watched Craig sleep as she accepted two very important things at that moment. One, she did love him. Second, that she could never be his wife. He deserved someone whole who could give him a family. He would be the most amazing father. And she could never be a mother.

Chapter Twenty

Craig groaned and hit the alarm, but the damn thing kept wailing, making him clench his jaw and sit up. The familiar anger settled between his eyes, took hold of his chest as he took in the empty bedroom. His empty bedroom. His empty life.

Dammit. What was that fucking noise?

He rolled out of bed in search of the phone that must be in the other room.

He ran a hand down his rough face, noted the ED number, and answered.

"Doctor," his colleague chirped into his weary brain. He dropped into a chair and listened to her, recalling the moment he realized she had the hots for him and had been flirting her ass off for months, trying to get his attention.

Lynn Park was a slight woman, but not one to be underestimated. She had more innate smarts, common medical sense and energy packed into her slight frame than an entire department full of doctors.

He put a hand over his eyes, remembering their quick encounter a few nights ago, after a long, stressful shift. He'd been staring at the wall, barely seeing anything for the exhaustion coursing through him. She'd put a hand on his shoulder, and he'd been tempted to kiss her. He'd reached for her. Pulled her close. But stopped himself.

Things had been a mess ever since. She kept her distance, and he felt like a shit. Made for a lovely work atmosphere.

Not.

His frustration at Suzanne's withdrawal from him over the last half-year had reached a fever pitch. He loved the woman to distraction, but was within days of telling her to take her emotional constipation and shove it. He couldn't take it anymore. He rose from the seat where he'd been half dozing, half cursing his current love life situation when Dr. Park ran into the break room.

"It's Rob Freitag, Craig. He's in the ER and his, erm, the woman that, ah..."

"Lila." He started pulling on scrubs he'd just abandoned a few hours before. "Is she in labor?"

"Yeah, I sent her up to OB but Rob's here too, and he's in terrible shape."

"I'm on my way."

By the time he made it back to the emergency department that had become his second home, the familiar sights, sounds and smells invigorated him. Made him realize why he'd gone to medical school. He bypassed the triage area and ran back to the curtains, finding Rob in the middle of a horrific coughing fit. Lynn was there with him, her stethoscope pressed to his back, her eyes dark with concern.

Nurses had hooked up IV's and were injecting, what Craig hoped, were painkillers. The guy didn't have much hope left unless a donor was found, and that was a one in a million shot at this point. He took a set of vitals and made sure he was resting as the morphine eased into his bloodstream.

"The baby. Lila. Is everyone okay?" Rob's voice was so breathy, Craig had a hard time hearing him. He put the oxygen mask back over the man's mouth and nose.

"I'll check, I promise, and get right back to you. Leave this on, Rob. You need it."

Rob nodded, shut his eyes, and Craig watched his chest rise and fall, realizing the effort the man's body was making just to get at that life giving air. He grabbed his phone and sent Suzanne a text out of habit. Not thinking she'd make the effort to come here, not after their last huge blow-out fight. But knowing Rob was her friend, she'd want to know what was going on with him.

He walked past the main ER desk without a word to anyone, hit floor seven in the elevator and leaned back against the wall, exhausted in body and mind. The words he and Suzanne had thrown at each most recently other flashed across his memory banks, making him wince.

"Stop looking for another excuse to push me away."

"I don't need an excuse, Craig. It just won't work."

"But I... you... we... Jesus, woman. We love each other. Why is that not enough for you? It's plenty for me."

She'd kept her back to him, ignoring him. He'd yanked her around harder than he meant to. But the look in her eyes wasn't fear. It was resolve.

"Just go," she ground out. "You and Blake both thought you could fix me. Well you can't, okay? I'm damaged. I'll always be damaged. I can't have children. I can't give you anything resembling a normal family life."

He'd gripped her arms, stared into her eyes. "I don't need kids, Suzanne. How many times do I have to say this for you to believe me? Why won't you listen?"

They'd stood, both of them breathing heavily, the putrid smoke of unspoken words coiling between them. "You say that. But you don't mean it. I know you Craig. You will be an amazing father. But you can't with me, don't you get it?. So go. Here. Take this." She'd tried to hand him the necklace, but he'd stepped away from her, fury blinding him and making him say stupid shit.

"You know what? You're right. You are damaged. Beyond repair, it seems. Or maybe you just aren't willing to be woman enough to own up the fact that a man loves you for you—not for your potential as a baby maker or for your supposed normalcy. That's sad and getting old. Stop feeling sorry for yourself, Suzanne. And maybe, just maybe, someday someone will stick around longer than me, so you can be happy."

"Craig," she'd said, tears standing in her eyes. But he held up a hand.

"I think you should go on living your pity party. I don't want to hear it anymore. If you can't see what's right in front of you—what has been right in front of you for six years now, well, I give. Uncle. I'm done." He'd stomped out, gone to The Local and gotten shitfaced. The estimable and saintly Blake himself had made him drink two glasses of water before pulling him off his barstool.

"Fuck you, get off me," he'd tried to shake the guy off, pissed but not even sure why.

"I know what you're going through, man."

"No, you don't." Craig had let Blake stuff him into a Lyft. He'd made a valiant attempt to focus on the man's face as he leaned into the open window.

"Yeah, Craig. I do. But stick with it. She's worth it."

The elevator door opened onto the women's center, jarring him from ugly memory lane. He walked out to the desk, asked about Lila's condition. Blake, eyes red rimmed and face haggard, was leaning against the wall outside one of the birthing rooms. The distinct sound of a newborn baby floated out from behind the door.

"Hey." He'd put a hand on Blake's shoulder. This whole thing was going to get way worse before it got better. He knew it. "Well?" He nodded to the door.

Blake's face collapsed, and he slid to the floor, back against the wall, face in his hands. Craig crouched down in front of him. But Blake looked up at him, smiling through his tears. "A boy," he whispered. "We have a son." Craig pulled him to his feet, and they went into the room together.

• • • •

JACK HUSTLED SUZANNE to the door, his phone to his ear, after helping her close on the sale of her Barton Hills house. He ended the call and grabbed her arm. "Hey, can you come with me to the hospital? I could use some moral support."

She took a breath. She knew the facts. Rob was dying. Craig had called her late just last night, lifting her heart at the sound of his voice but reducing her to tears with his words. He'd told her everything.

Including the fact that Rob and Blake and Lila had decided to take Rob home.

Tears streaked her face as she followed Jack over to the U of M medical center. Her heart broke at the thought of what Blake was dealing with. He had been through so much. It was incomprehensible, especially considering the baby—Gabriel Robert— was only two weeks old.

When they walked out of the elevator, she spotted Craig right away. He came to her, gave her a squeeze. "I'm sorry honey," he said into her hair, then let her go.

The feel of his arms around her set off the waterworks yet again. She leaned on Rob's hospital room door, taking it all in. Blake, sitting by Rob's head on one side, rubbing his lips with ice cubes. Lila, looking haunted, nursing the baby with tears running down her cheeks. She shuddered and leaned into Jack when he came up behind her.

"Jesus, why is this happening to our friend?"

He held her until she cried herself out then handed her a tissue when she let go of his shirt. Blake—the man who'd saved her in more ways than one — stood in front of her, his green eyes haunted. But he held out his arms, and she went into them, wrapping her arms around his waist.

"Don't let him go," he whispered into her hair before releasing her to Craig, who had walked up behind them. "He's everything I wasn't, and he loves you. Don't blow this one." He walked away, his shoulder slumped, his hands jammed into his jeans pockets.

Suzanne would replay that split second in her mind over and over again in the months to come. Wishing it back, wishing she'd said something, anything, to him to remind him he'd been right for her once, too. That she'd released him to his new life with nothing but good intentions, at a high cost to herself.

She flinched when Craig slipped his arm around her waist. But intense relief rolled through her at his presence. She shut her eyes. He kissed her hair, making her shiver. She opened them and saw Jack and Sara at the far end of the hall. Jack had their new baby in his arms. Suzanne felt her heart constrict, but she pressed herself closer to Craig. He tightened his grip on her. "I miss you," he whispered.

They stood together, watching as Sara and Blake's parents joined the group. "Want to go see him?" he asked her. She nodded. Craig took her hand and led her down the hallway.

She forced herself to smile at the sight of her friend, tried to suppress a gasp of dismay at the sight of his gaunt face and blue lips. He held out an arm and she let him hold her. "Damn you Freitag." She let the tears fall. Craig fussed around Rob's IV, listened to his chest, but Rob brushed him away.

"Spare me Doc. Just let me go home."

Suzanne held back a sob. Craig put a hand on Rob's shoulder. "All right, I'm trying to facilitate it. But the protocols...."

"Yeah, yeah." Rob kissed Suzanne's cheek, then pushed her away. Her knees shook so hard she thought she might fall over.

"I'll go check on the paperwork." Craig tugged her out of the room with him. Lila went back in with the baby.

Blake was crouched down on the floor right outside Rob's room, his head in his arms. She could tell he was about to come apart at the seams. His natural tendency was to be high energy, never sitting still, and she realized he must have used up so much of it fighting for the man he loved, trying to find solutions, cures, anything. She joined him on the floor, kissed his cheek, and kept her mouth shut. She'd long ago relinquished her right to give him advice about anything.

"Thanks," he said, rubbing his hands across his face before rising and going back inside the room. Craig pulled her up and led her to a seat, gave her a quick brush of his lips before heading to the nurse's station. Jack sank into the chair nearby, jiggling his mewling infant. She smiled and held out her arms without a word. She smiled down at him as he jiggled around, yawned, then treated her to such a brilliant, blue-eyed grin her heart pounded.

"Jesus." Jack ran a hand down his face. She looked down the hall, catching sight of Sara talking with her parents. When the Doctors Thornton joined them, Blake's mother's eyes were red-rimmed, but she was holding it together. Matthew channeled his frustration into bossiness—demanding to talk to oncologists, trying to wrangle the potential, non-existent transplant.

Beth put a hand on her husband's shoulder. "Honey, you're not helping." He sat, leaning elbows on his knees, then jumped to his feet when Blake strode down the hall.

He stopped in front of his parents and sister. "I'm gonna head over and pick up Katie and Maddie. I'll take everybody home and get them settled. Lila and Gabe will come with Rob in the ambulance." Suzanne had never seen him look so helpless. She focused her gaze down at baby Brandis to keep from bursting into tears.

"Okay honey. We'll be by later. We'll spell you guys with Gabe," Blake's mother said, her voice steady. Suzanne watched Blake's father grip his arms, then pull him close for a fierce hug. Blake's eyes shone with emotion as he pulled away.

"Thanks," he said, then turned and headed for the elevators. Jack took the now sleeping baby from her arms and settled him into his seat. She looked around for Craig, but must have been called back to the ED. She fiddled with her phone, sent Evan a text update and drank some dreadful swill they claimed was coffee and waited some more.

She dozed, waking to the sound of Sara's aggravated voice.

"Where the hell is Blake? Julie just called. He's not there yet."

Jack tried to talk to her, but she jerked out of his grip. When she answered another call, her eyes darkened with concern and she stalked away from the group. The whole thing unrolled before Suzanne's eyes like a silent movie montage the split second before disaster—and a sense of eerie dread settled deep in Suzanne's chest. But was no wonder.

They were about to lose a good friend and they all had to watch it happen. She sighed and stretched her legs out on an adjoining seat.

Craig dealt with the myriad crises demanded of him as second in command of a major university emergency department, but his mind remained upstairs with Suzanne. She'd felt so good to him. And damn him if he weren't glad something had forced her back to his side. God he was such a fucking sap. He missed her so much it was a physical ache.

She sent him a text to ask about Rob's transport home. And then a second time, telling him that Sara was freaking out because no one had heard from Blake. He realized it had been almost two hours since the man had left to pick up his niece, Katie, and Lila's daughter, Maddie, and get them home ahead of Rob.

He ignored the worry and focused on the facts. A gunshot wound call came in on the intercom. He rallied the staff, did his usual prep. But let Lynn take the lead, as a hot nugget of anxiety began to bloom in his chest. When Suzanne sent him another "where's Blake" message, he was hanging out by the radio, determined that he was worried for no reason.

Then he heard it. The call that changed everything.

He grabbed the handset, barked out a few questions, willing himself to remain calm. This couldn't be happening.

But it was. And it was his job to deal with it first.

He paged the transplant team on autopilot. The paramedics had called in the horrific car accident quickly enough for Craig to tell them to keep the man they'd pulled from the wreckage, breathing. That he was a potential donor. Trying to like hell to hold it together, he grabbed his phone and called the one guy he trusted to help him relay the news. Jack answered, his voice gruff and angry.

"What the fuck is going on, Doc?"

Craig opened his mouth, and the words "Blake is dead but ..." were about to pass his lips when Jack stopped him.

"Can you come up here?" Jack muttered over what sounded like a shriek of dismay nearby. Craig squeezed his eyes shut, then opened them when he heard the ambulance pull up.

"I have to stay. He's, um, his ambulance just got here. The transplant team is on its way. They'll need signatures. Are his parents...."

"No, they left. Why is... oh shit. What happened?"

"It's Blake. He was in a car accident. I'm keeping him alive long enough to..."

Craig took a breath and rallied his calm voice. "Call your in-laws, Jack. I can get Sara to sign the order required to take his lungs, but Beth and Matthew need to get back here now."

Suzanne's half-awake dreams had the odd, floating, half-awake quality she remembered from her days in medical school. The sound of a familiar female voicing yelling "no" over and over made her eyes snap open. She jumped up, trying to sort out who was screaming. Her eyes saw, but couldn't take it in at first. Jack cradled his wife as she sat on the floor against the wall, shaking her head, screaming the word "no." Nurses rushed at her but Jack held them off and got Sara to her feet, holding her close and whispering in her ear. The look of utter agony on the woman's tear stained face sent a bolt of terror through Suzanne's chest.

The elevator dinged open.

Craig. Thank God.

She ran to him, but he held her off, looking around for someone else. There were three somber-looking doctors with him, one of them holding a tablet and a stylus for signing. Craig finally looked at her. Fear flared in Suzanne's chest.

"Rob? Is he...?"

But Craig shook his head and zeroed in on Sara. Suzanne watched as if from a million miles away. He spoke words that made her heart seize up, then turned her entire body into a block of ice.

Blake. Dear God. How could it be? It was supposed to be Rob.

Sara shook, but Jack helped her sign the tablet before she collapsed back to the floor. He stood as nurses moved in with needles, and guided Sara to an empty room. Her old friend looked up and met her eyes, shook his head and turned away.

Lila emerged from Rob's room, rubbing her face. The cadre of doctors moved towards her. She started backing away. Jack took Lila's arm and said something Suzanne couldn't hear. Her hearing seemed off, buzzy, as if shutting down in denial of what had happened. Jack led Lila back into Rob's room. Suzanne sank into a chair, and let the reality wash over her like a tidal wave.

A hand dropped on her shoulder. She looked up and the sight of Craig's deep brown eyes broke something loose in her. She choked out a sob, and he held her close. The sounds of the hospital rolled around them as they stood, clutching each other. She felt fury build in her, anger at all the people around them who were still alive. Because the one man loved by so many was dead in the flash of chrome and screech of tires.

Craig gripped her arms and held her away from him. She tried to catch a breath, focus on his words. When they coalesced, it lit a flame in her brain. "God damn you, Suzanne. Marry me. Please. I can't lose you."

She gasped, tore herself out his arms. His eyes were dark, his shoulders hunched. "What the hell are you talking about?"

"Us. You and me. Together. I'm sick of playing this stupid game with you. We are happy together. I need you to admit it. I need you." He looked positively frantic.

She stared at him as the sounds of abject agony hit her ears. Sara was still crying as she fought the sedative they'd given her. Then she saw Lila, being propped up by Jack.

"We're going down...to see him." Lila said when she was close enough for them to hear her whisper. Jack held onto her and looked at Craig.

"They're moving Rob to the OR. And he's out anyway. So she wanted to...Christ." Jack's voice broke.

Lila gripped her arm, startling her. "Do you want to come with us?"

Suzanne stared at her, unwilling to acknowledge what the woman was asking of her. Her teeth chattered. Craig held onto her.

"You don't have to," he whispered in her ear, but she pulled away, still furious with him, and at herself, for being such a cold bitch in the face of his earnest emotional reaction to the horrible moment. He stepped back, his face closing down.

A small voice told her this was it. She'd pushed him away one time too many. But she turned to Lila, held the woman up on her other side.

"I'll go with you."

Jack shot her a grateful look. She took a breath. Together they headed to the operating room where Blake's lungs were being removed. Lila's face was a rictus of horror and disbelief. But when Suzanne saw him, his beautiful face unrecognizable from the accident, her heart calmed. He was doing what he'd want to do—he was going to save Rob's life.

The organ harvest team finished and nodded to their small group indicating they could come in. Suzanne reached out a trembling hand. "Good bye," she said brushing his hair back. She put her lips to his ruined cheek, then felt Jack's hand on her arm pulling her away. She didn't remember much after that.

Chapter Twenty-One

Eighteen Months Later

Suzanne stared at the spreadsheets in front of her. Heard and smelled the brewery functioning all around, but registered little else. Her head pounded from lack of sleep. Her hands shook as she tried to focus.

It was no use.

She pushed back from the desk, spent yet more energy dispelling Blake from her memory banks. Evan walked into the back office, reaming someone out on the phone, but her vision was dim, like it had been for months. The air had gone out of her since Blake's accident. Not because the man was hers to lose, but because on that day, she'd driven a nail into the coffin of her own relationship with Craig.

She ignored Evan when he dropped into a chair opposite her huge metal desk and ended his call. She'd been ignoring everyone for a while, anyway. The entire place had gone into a state of shock when the news hit about their onetime young brewer dying in a car accident.

Suzanne's eyes burned, the ubiquitous tears threatening once again. She put her head on her arms, rested them on the desk and wished for the thousandth time that she'd said more to him that last day.

She jumped a mile when Evan touched her arm. "Hey." He seemed to want to say more. But didn't.

"You look like shit," she muttered, taking in the dark circles under his eyes, the exhaustion etched into the lines on his face.

He shrugged. "The girls are having a growth spurt. Up all night, eating all the time. You know."

She stared at him, her brain registering that he assumed she would know. She looked away, realizing that he had meant nothing by it. Craig was right. She had to stop being so sensitive. She squeezed her eyes shut.

Craig. Dear God, she missed him.

She fiddled with her phone, avoiding Evan's gaze, scrolled back through a recent text conversation they'd shared—nothing more than an information exchange about Sara and Jack's collective frame of mind a year after the tragedy.

"She seems ok." Craig written when she had asked.

"He doesn't." She was worried about her friend. He'd withdrawn from pretty much everything while staying focused on his stupid soccer project. Otherwise absent, but for his physical presence.

"Yeah. I know. She's in denial, I think. Not really dealing with it other than helping everyone else. A departure for her."

"Well, maybe that's his problem," she'd written. "He's used to being the strong one. If she doesn't need him to be or is in denial about it. Then he may feel…" She'd stopped, unsure what to say, and hit send.

She stared at the words, willing the man back to her, but realizing her last rejection of him had been the final straw for him, and she had no one to blame but herself for the result.

He was logical and calm. His wild, irrational proposal that terrible day had scared her, but she'd sleepwalked through the next couple of weeks and never answered him. Together, they observed the excruciating aftermath. Saw Rob a day after he woke and got the news. Then relived the whole thing all over again with him. It had been a gut-churning exercise for everyone concerned.

She sighed, kept reading the conversation, happy at least to have these written words of his.

"He feels useless," Craig had said. "And a guy like Jack can't feel that way without taking action. I guess his action in this case is to back away from her. Let her handle it however she will."

"But what about the baby? He must love having him around." Suzanne had forced herself to type that out.

"Sara thinks he's having some kind of freak-out relative to having a son. Because his father was such a shit, or something."

"Well, Gordon Senior was a shit. Damn. Poor guy."

"Yeah. Poor all of them." He'd written. Then, about a second later, these words had popped up on her screen in the little blue chat bubble: "Poor me. Poor us."

That had given her pause. She hadn't known how to respond, so she didn't, leaving the conversation dangling like their on-again-off-again, seemingly doomed relationship.

Later that night, he'd sought her out online. She cursed herself for leaving her google chat live, but smiled despite herself at his message. "What? You didn't want to join my pity party?"

She answered, hoping to sound brisk and matter of fact. "Well, I know how I must have sounded. Point taken."

His response was swift. "Good. About the point, I mean."

"Yeah. Is there anything else? I need to get to bed."

She stared at the blinky "Craig is writing" bubbles. Wishing she had the intestinal fortitude to just cut the man off. To let him go. But she couldn't. His answer made her face split into a huge grin. "So. What are you wearing?"

"Are you flirting with me?" she'd typed, unsuccessfully holding back the longing that rose. Memories of his extraordinary talents at pleasing her made her breathless.

"I was sort of hoping to cut straight to the phone sex."

"Well, first off, we aren't using phones..."

"You're crueler than I thought."

She bit her lip, tried to decide how to respond. He pre-empted her. "Sara is a complete mess. I talked to her today. How's Jack, really?"

She frowned, made her brain flip a switch from horny enough to have computer chat sex to contemplating her friend's deteriorating home life.

"Worse, I'm willing to bet. He was at the bar last night. Drunk off his ass. I had to pour him into a Lyft home, making all sorts of threatening noises about not jeopardizing what he had. About not falling back into his bad habits."

"He won't cheat on her."

"Is that a question or a statement?" she answered.

"A statement. She isn't worried about that. Believe it or not."

"I believe it. They've reached common ground on the trust thing, I think. But this other thing he's doing. Withdrawing from her and the kids. That's worse at this point." She sighed, remembering her friend's harsh laughter, his unwillingness to talk to her the other night.

"So. What are you wearing?"

She laughed and responded. "Wow. That was fast."

"Sorry. Well?"

"We don't need to be doing this, Craig."

"What? Flirting? Why not? I mean, it's innocent. We know it's not going anywhere."

Her heart sank. "Well, in that case, I have on dirty sweat pants, a too-big tee shirt and my hair hasn't been washed for two days."

"Oh baby. You know how to make me hard."

"Shut up. I'm going to bed." But she didn't want to. She wanted more than anything to keep talking. She forced herself not to pick up the phone and call him, let his low, lovely singer's voice fill her ears.

"Tell me more about how nasty you look. I love it."

She grinned, her fingers hovering over the keys. She typed, "I love you," and hit send, willing it back within of half a second. She white knuckled her own hands for a solid five minutes. Then six, seven, and almost eight more minutes passed before he answered.

"Well, you know how I feel about you. I've told you enough."

"Yes. I do." Tears blurred her vision. "Is it too late? Can I take it all back?"

The response was immediate and final.

"Good night, my lovely ginger girl. Sleep tight."

His chat icon blinked then went dark.

Craig sat straight up, his reflexes honed after years of medical school, internships, and residencies to function at a high level from a dead sleep. The dark room wouldn't reveal what noise had caused him to wake.

He put his hand down, reaching for Suzanne. When he found a female form beside him, his brain clicked in, causing buckets of guilt and remorse to pour over his psyche.

No, it wasn't Suzanne. Not the woman he wanted.

Lynn stirred, rolled over, and tugged him back down. Her sleepy exhalations and warm, naked presence made his body go on autopilot. Anger shut out logic. Bright, blinding fury at himself for pulling this innocent woman into the middle of his mess, misleading her into thinking their near constant fuck sessions meant anything more to him than that.

He kissed her with a ferocity born of frustration. His brain fuzzed over. Lynn's welcoming body soothed him, but even as he came, her near operatic climax deafening him, he whispered Suzanne's name.

Later, he sat at the kitchen table sipping coffee and staring into the middle distance. When Lynn wandered in, fresh from a shower, she said nothing. Just filled her travel mug and leaned on the sink. As if in slow motion, he rose and pulled her to him. He sighed and held her close. She didn't move. "I'm sorry," he muttered. "Don't go."

She pulled away, smiled at him, her eyes resigned as she tugged her long black hair into a pony tail. "Gotta go save some lives."

Craig felt like the worst kind of shithead. He'd made an idiot of himself begging Suzanne to marry him. She'd rejected him, of course. For the last time, he'd resolved. If something as bad as losing such an important member of their odd, yet close-knit circle, didn't make her realize they owed it to themselves to be together—to be happy—well, then, screw her.

So he had.

Well, he'd screwed Lynn. That very night.

A lot.

Lynn claimed she understood. That she wanted nothing more from him than what he was giving her. But he refused to be That Guy. He felt terrible about his own inability to stop channeling his grief over the loss of Suzanne by diving between his colleague's thighs.

"Craig." She snapped her fingers in front of his eyes. Then slid into the seat across from him, perched there as if about to launch into the atmosphere—like she always did. "I think we should, um, cool it a while."

He looked away from her, the yawning empty nights without her to distract him from his misery a terrifying concept. He reached out and grabbed her hand, words falling from his lips he knew he'd regret. "No. I don't want to cool it. I want... I need you. Move in with me."

She bit her lip. A single tear slid down her cheek. "Craig. You don't want me. I know it. You know it. It's not fair. So, I'm gonna go."

He watched her, paralyzed, as she grabbed the few items of clothing she'd left lying around in the past few months and opened the condo door. She stopped, looked back at him once, her face a mask of sympathy tinged with real unhappiness.

"I'm sorry, Lynn," he blurted out. He wanted to stand and yank her back. But something made him stop. He realized it was her eyes. They were hard, firm, and set.

"I know you are. I'm sorry, too. But, I can't live like this. I love you. And you... don't. So, I'm going. Don't call me anymore."

And like that, she was gone.

His vision darkened. Fury boiled in him. An unwelcome need to punch something made him clench his fists. His heart pounded. For a split second, he thought he might be having a heart attack. He sat, clasped his hands together in front of him, and forced himself to be calm.

It took almost an hour for him to get his head around a single concept — he would never find true happiness. He'd could never quite seem to get the timing right, or the woman right, or the combination of the two at the same time.

Suzanne had been right about a lot of things, but all the accusations about him wanting or deserving a family, of wanting to be a father, had been dead wrong. He honestly didn't care. But he'd given up convincing her of that. Now, it would seem, he'd ruined yet another potential relationship by not letting go of the previous one. He put his head down, the cool glass tabletop easing the heat in his face.

His phone buzzed with a text. Suzanne's name popped up, but he grabbed the damn thing and heaved it against the tile backsplash, making a satisfying mess before realizing that he'd left the phone he used to communicate with the busy Michigan emergency department in the glove box of his truck.

"Fuck!"

He yelled it again, then again for good measure as he hit the elevator button and went down to the cavernous parking garage to retrieve it. Bracing himself on the wood handles all the way down, and berating himself for be a sap, a pushover, and a dumbass the entire way.

Chapter Twenty-Five

It was a solid month before he saw Suzanne again. To her credit, she'd not called, texted or emailed him either, after the morning of the destroyed phone incident.

He sat by the pool after a traumatic day at work and an hour-long workout, chest heaving. The memories crashing in him came close to drowning him with their intensity.

It was simple enough to avoid Lynn since he made the schedule and never had them crossing paths. His body had eased away from its skin-crawling need to fuck all the time which had gripped him during the couple of months Lynn had been obliging him by taking the edge off. And falling in love with him in the process.

The bone-deep sorrow remained. His chest ached when he thought about Suzanne, no matter what he did.

But he carried on. He did his job. Saved lives. He swam like a motherfucker — lap after lap after lap, pushing himself so hard it was all he could do to pull himself out of the pool on trembling arms. Like now, sitting there on the pool's edge, watching the moon cast an eerie glow over the water. Remembering. First Sara, there, with him, but not really.

Then Suzanne, who'd spent hours swimming laps alongside him.

She'd dropped into his life at such an odd time. The way they'd hit it off, her easy, breezy manner at first disguising her inner unhappiness. How he'd taken the task of making her happy, with him, to heart. How he had, for a while. Until she'd flip out over the whole family or baby thing.

He ran a shaking hand down his face at the same time he realized he hadn't eaten since the night before. Groaning, he got to his feet, made his wobbly way back to the towel stand, and almost plowed right over her.

She stood in the shadows near the small locker room door. Her petite frame seemed even more so, her eyes huge, face gaunt. She gripped her elbows, bit her lip. He stumbled, caught himself, and stepped away from her. Anger made his jaw ache.

"How did you get in here?"

She sucked in a breath and squared her shoulders. His heart started a slow meltdown, a thaw the likes of which made him shiver, and that made his cock instantly hard. He wrapped a towel around his waist and put more distance between them.

"I miss you." Her words spoke volumes. But he wasn't about to go there again.

"Really." He dropped to a chair, wincing at the tightness in his swimsuit. "Oh, well." He attempted nonchalance. Her face revealed nothing but unhappiness. He steeled himself against it.

"Don't, Craig. This is hard enough."

He couldn't help himself or hold back the derisive snort. "You're telling me how hard this is? That's gutsy."

She took a step towards him, but he backed away, stumbling a bit as he kept the chair between them. The hand she'd been using to reach for him shook. A wave of forgiving remorse tried to bowl him over. But he hardened himself against it.

No. He wouldn't cave. Not again.

"Leave my condo key on the table on your way out." He turned away. She moved fast, surprising him, darting around the chair as if they were playing tag and wrapping her arms around his neck, going up on her tiptoes to reach his lips. But he turned his head. "I won't be played, Suzanne. I can't. Jesus. That poor bastard Blake. Now I know how he felt."

She jumped back as if he'd struck her. The sadness in her eyes flipped to anger. He crossed his arms. They stood, fury swirling between them.

"You have no idea how he felt. It's my fault I keep projecting my relationship with him onto us. I... deserved that."

"Yeah, I know. It's why I said it." His teeth ground together. He forced himself to stop. To settle his face into neutral "who gives a shit" lines. It was harder than it looked.

She swallowed hard, looked down, then back up into his eyes, making his pulse race.

"I realized something this week." She took a seat, leaving just a few inches between them. As a defensive mechanism, he sat, increasing the space. For his own good. The need to sweep her into his arms, to quell the increasing agony in her eyes with one kiss, very nearly overwhelmed him.

"What? That you're an emotionally stunted grown woman hiding behind the screen of abuse by a guy who is not me to keep from realizing that you do love me?" He spoke to the ceiling. Not caring if she heard him or not. Then he met her gaze.

She glared at him. But her face shifted, and she smiled. He mirrored her, unable to stop. "Cut that out," he forced himself to sound pissed.

"Cut what out?"

He leaned back, bringing fresh blood to his already aching cock. "I'm righteously indignant. And I'm not taking you back. So just stop trying." He rose, but she put a hand on his knee.

He made a half-hearted attempt to stand and escape her, but with a strength he didn't realize she had, she pushed him down onto his back. She straddled him, propping herself on the lounge chair arms. Her eyes were dark. It took everything he had not to yank her down, to fuck her silly. To not communicate, but to connect.

She thumbed his chin. "I need you. Can I get a mulligan?"

"No. You can't. Seriously, Suzanne. Just get the hell out."

She got to her feet and with a couple of quick movements stood before him, utterly naked. He groaned, and put a hand over his eyes, tried to force out the image burned into his retinas—the porcelain flawlessness of her skin, the hard peaks of her dark pink nipples, the red hair she'd let grow, curving around her face, and the light dusting of fire covering her sex.

He opened his eyes at the splash. She cut through the water with ease, her lithe form moving the way he'd taught her all those times they'd spent here together. He curled his hands into fists. Got to his feet, his head light from lack of blood and cock aching from an overabundance of it.

In a daze, he tugged his suit down, stepped out of it and dove in the deep end, loving the way the cool water caressed his skin. They passed each other again and again. He focused on moving his body, not grabbing her like he wanted to do. After a while, he lost track of time. There was nothing but the water, the sounds in his ears, the smell in his nose, his muscles trembling with too little protein and too much exertion. He grabbed the side, leaned on his arms, and tried to catch his breath.

Her touch made him shiver, but he didn't care. Not anymore. He moved in front of her, braced himself on either side of her, propping her under her arms.

"No fair." He exhaled before slanting his mouth over her. Losing himself in her scent, her sounds, hating himself but unable to stop.

Suzanne's entire body hummed, her ears were fuzzy and still half-full of water. When he faced her, propped her with his arms and stared into her eyes, she experienced a glimmer of hope. A small corner of maybe that she nestled into needing it so much she wanted to cry.

He blew out a puff of air. Closed his eyes as if denying what he was about to do. "No fair," he sighed into her mouth. The touch of his lips to hers was more perfect than it had ever been. In all the many moments of intimacy they'd shared, this one seemed like destiny.

Don't be a hysteric Victorian over dramatizing everything.

But oh, how much she missed him.

She wrapped her entire body around him. Arms, legs, lips, tongues, teeth, all tangled in an urgent swirl. She gasped, loving the sensation of his length at the sudden tilt and thrust of his hips. She exhaled and arched into him. "Oh... god," she said in relief.

"Still just me." He pulled out slowly, teasing her, then shoved in high and hard, never taking his eyes from hers. A tear fell. He kissed it away, his lips soft, in distinct contrast to his lower body which had taken on an edge of urgency. She met him thrust for thrust, dug her fingers into his shoulders.

"Harder," she whispered.

He flipped around so he was leaning against the wall. Put his hands on her hips and ground against her before threading a hand in her hair and yanking her face to his. "Is this it then?" His voice rough. His lips were so firm, his tongue so damn delicious. "One last fuck?"

She broke away, lifted, and slid back down onto his shaft. The orgasm hovered, just out of reach. Her brain tried to shut down, but she was so happy to be here, back with him. Reasons and motivations be damned. This was where she belonged, and she could admit it. "I love you. So much Craig. Please."

She wrapped her arms around his head, held him close as he took one of her nipples between his lips. Sucked hard, dragging that orgasm kicking and screaming out into the light of day. She groaned as her body shuddered and her vision dimmed. The sheer rightness, the utter completeness that crawled up her spin, settling in behind her eyes making them leak yet more of the infernal tears.

"Gonna come. I'm... Jesus." When he came inside her, no image of an unattainable baby made her want to cry. A different vision spilled into her brain.

She and Craig, together. Just the two of them.

His hips kept moving against her. Their bodies stayed intertwined. He met her lips, kissed her, but just as she was about to wind her fingers in his hair, he lifted her up and off him, then swam away a few feet. She held onto the side, a sudden panic in her chest. "Craig," she said. "I love you."

He lifted himself out of the water. Giving her a full glimpse of the lean, tone of his body. His silence scared her. She leaned on the side, chin on her hands, watching him. "Did you hear me or are you—"

He whirled on her, his dark eyes unfathomable, which told her all she needed to know. "No, I'm not ignoring you." He dropped back into the seat.

She climbed out, the reticence she'd used for so long with him slipping back into place. She frowned at herself.

Stop it Suzanne. Don't hold back. This is your last chance.

She wrapped a towel around herself and stood in front of him. Expecting him to hold out his arms to her, she reminded herself that she deserved this. Every minute of his cold shoulder she had earned, in spades. She slipped onto his lap and buried her nose in his neck. "I do know. But I want this. I want to make it work."

He shoved her to the seat, off his lap, surprising her with his roughness. She frowned at his back, still trying to remain humble, to make amends for her bullshit. So many years of holding him off. Of making his dark eyes hurt. Of disappointing him. She wrapped her arms around her knees, at a loss.

"Does it matter that I want this? That I'm sorry? That I love you?"

He shouldered his way into the locker room without a word. She bit her lip. By the time he'd emerged, she'd redressed. He put his hands on his now jeans clad hips. She resisted the urge to go to him. To lick the line of pool water that dripped from his hair onto his neck.

"It matters." He kept his voice low. "Just like it mattered to you. How much I loved you. How many times I said it. How much I tried to convince you that you were exactly what I wanted."

She sucked in a breath. But he held up a hand. "Let me finish." He closed the gap between them, gripped her arms and kissed her, bringing light to the edges of her vision. She gasped when he tore his lips away. "But I don't think we can do this. I have to … I need … someone who loves me not because she feels sorry for herself or for me. But because she really, truly loves me."

"I do… I—"

He put two fingers over her lips, cutting her off.

"No. You don't. But I had fun and all." His dark eyes were cold, but it was nothing compared to the moment when he turned and left her there, alone. Without another word or even a backward glance.

Suzanne lay in the bed for almost a half second too long. She lurched up and stumbled into the bathroom of her small downtown condo. The room spun, the floor seemed to rise and meet her. She clutched at the toilet for dear life and let the contents of her stomach empty. Once it seemed she was finished, she groaned and rinsed her mouth out.

Waiting for the room to settle, she did a mental recount of the booze from the night before. It was no real surprise she'd lost her cookies. She'd sat with Evan and Julie and a bunch of Tap Room regulars the night before and consumed way too much beer, then switched to bourbon much too late for grown ups.

Typically, after a quick hurl, she could throw it off. That quick hurl happened, like three hours ago. She couldn't seem to stop. She gulped water straight from the faucet, trying to ease her severely dry mouth.

The floor of the bathroom had never looked so comfy. She slid down the wall, gathered a towel in her arms, and cried. By the time she got past that sudden burst of emotion, she hauled herself to her feet. After wobbling her way into the kitchen, she choked down a few saltines and made some weak tea.

Her phone rang, but she ignored it after assessing it was once again, not Craig. He refused to return her calls, her emails, anything. She had well and truly blown it. Their paths never crossed. She worked on autopilot most days, growing the brewery sales, doing her job. Came home and collapsed after sending yet one more unanswered email to him.

The fierce determination that had fueled her was fading. And she hated it. Jack texted her.

"Hey. Can you talk?"

She grabbed the phone, in no mood for Gordon drama.

"No."

He called within seconds. "What?"

"What's wrong?"

"Oh, you know, I tossed away the most amazing man in the universe. Twice. And he won't return my calls."

"Ah, the esteemed doctor."

"Yeah. So I go to my original question—what do you want?"

"Want me to talk to him?"

"Jesus, Jack, no. Stay out of it. You have your own issues."

"Um, well, okay." He stayed silent a few beats.

"Okay." She shut her eyes. "You and Sara are—"

"Working through it. We went away for a week, got a break from the kids. We fought some, but made up a lot. The usual. But things are better."

His voice sounded steady for the first time in months. She smiled. "Things all set for the memorial weekend, right?"

"Yeah, I have B&B names and—"

"I already know where I can stay." She shut her eyes to block the onrush of memories.

"All right. You and the good doctor, if you want him to be there."

She sighed, rose and had to run to the bathroom as the few bites of food she'd ingested made a sudden reappearance. "I gotta go," she choked out. "I'll be there."

It was a close-run thing, but she made it to the toilet just in time.

She brushed her teeth, trying not to gag on toothpaste, and wiped her face. Her eyes were sunk in their sockets, her face pale. She looked like shit and felt just as bad.

When the doorbell rang, she almost jumped a mile. Then made her slow way across the living room and peered through the peephole at an unfamiliar couple standing in the hall. She opened the door, ordering herself to not be sick all over their shoes.

"Hi, can I help you?

"Yes, Hi. Sorry to barge in on you." The woman held out a hand. "I'm Lillian. Craig's sister-in-law."

Suzanne's shoulders slumped as she took in the tall blonde-haired, dark-eyed man next to her who could be none other than Craig's brother. "Hi, I'm Rick," he said. His lopsided grin looked exactly like Craig's.

"Come in." She held the door open, more than a little freaked out by their appearance.

They sat in awkward silence, hands wrapped around glasses of iced tea. Her gorge kept threatening to rise, but she held it back and listened. "Um, so, what brings you to Ann Arbor?" she asked biting back the urge to ask the "How the hell do you know where I live" half of that question.

Rick leaned on the table, pinning her with a set of very familiar brown eyes. "Okay, so small talk seems like a waste of time. We came here to tell you one thing. That I love my brother. And he is miserable. And.. well." Rick rubbed the back of her neck. The effort to not puke took all her energy, so Suzanne stayed quiet.

Lillian spoke next, putting a cool hand on Suzanne's arm. "He loves you. A lot. He's told me over the years." She grabbed Suzanne's hand, startling her. "I'm so sorry for all you've been through."

Lillian leaned forward, keeping Suzanne's hand in a death grip. "Don't hurt him. I mean, he's not perfect and god knows a lot of that is our fault, but... he's special, you know?" Suzanne nodded, still speechless. "We were sent here as ambassadors for the family. To tell you that you need to stop being so stubborn. Love him back."

Suzanne gulped. "I've tried. He doesn't seem interested in me anymore. And I can't blame him."

Lillian's gaze narrowed. "Oh, he is. But he's doing his own stubborn dance. You can't give up. He needs you."

Rick leaned back in his chair. "Listen, Suzanne, we spoiled that kid. I mean, he was like everyone's baby. And while we've ruined him on some levels, I like to think we trained him better—you know—to be a good partner."

"Did you guys come all the way to Michigan to talk to me?" The thought of having such a close-knit family that so many people cared about you enough to do something like this made her head buzzy.

Suzanne shot to her feet, the scene somehow making her nausea worse. "I'm pregnant," she blurted out. Tears ran down her cheeks. Lillian stood, held her close. How she knew this she had no idea, but it all made a strange sort of sense. She'd stopped counting on her body to do its job, to conceive and carry a child. But the thought that she and Craig had overcome it was terrifying, and somehow right.

Lillian held Suzanne at arm's length. "Go to him. Tell him. Be a family, but just..."

Suzanne shut her eyes. "I know. Love him. I do."

Rick rose and put an arm around his wife, then took Suzanne's hand. "You won't regret it, Suzanne. He needs you. And he will be a amazing father."

Craig pulled a double shift and was in zero mood for any human contact. But the sight of Sara standing at the door of his building made him smile. She held him close. He closed his eyes against the memories. And the anger.

She let go of him but held his arms, stared hard into his eyes. "What?" he asked. "I'm tired. Need sleep." But she wouldn't let go of him. "Sara, what is it? You ok? Jack is—"

She shook her head. "No, no. It's not about me. We wanted to make sure you were aware of the memorial we're having. Next weekend."

Craig took a breath. "Jesus. It's been two years, hasn't it?" He ran a hand across his face. Exhaustion permeated his every pore. "Come on up."

They ascended in silence. He headed for a shower, leaving Sara to her own devices. By the time he came back out, she'd made coffee, found some fruit and cheese, and sat reading a magazine at his kitchen table. He leaned in the doorway, rubbing his hair with a towel.

"You look good," he said, meaning it. He was one hundred percent over her, he knew. But it felt nice having her in his space as a friend.

She looked up at him, a smile spreading across her face. "Thanks. I'm feeling better." He slumped into the chair across from her, but pushed the steaming cup of coffee away.

"I can't drink another drop of this stuff. Double shift." He shrugged, accepted the grape and the piece of cheese she held up. "How's Katie? Brandis? Your life? I never see you anymore."

She ticked off her fingers as she spoke. "A smart mouth. A handful, when he's not a bottomless pit. Not too bad. I know."

He laughed at her irreverence, put a hand on her arm. "I'm a wreck, sorry."

"I heard."

He narrowed his eyes. "You heard what, exactly?"

"Things with Suzanne are on the outs again. What's up with her, anyway? You're a great guy."

She had the decency to blush when he almost fell out of his chair laughing. "Jesus," he sputtered. "I guess you'd know. You let me go too, remember?" He downed an enormous glass of water, trying not to let his emotions get the best of him. "I gotta get some sleep." He kept his eyes on the sink.

"Want me to talk to her?"

"No. Thanks. It's over. Nothing to salvage." His chest constricted, but he blew out a breath. He had to let it go.

"Well, anyway." She hugged him from behind, kissed his shoulder, and grabbed her keys from the counter. "Can you come? It would be great. I mean, if you guys can...."

"I'll be there. Not with her, but I'll be there."

Chapter Twenty-Six

The Memorial

Suzanne wished she could be anywhere else on the planet but here right now. Watching the little kids gather around Rob, sending their small boats out onto Lake Michigan, memorializing a man they had all lost, a light the world had lost, just two years ago.

Craig stood a few feet from her, sipping water, staring out over the water. He looked thinner. She sighed, sipped her ginger ale, trying to hold down the ever-present nausea. When she couldn't take his scrutiny anymore she walked over to Rob and put her hand on his shoulder. He stayed crouched on the lake shore, then looked up at her, his eyes bright with tears. She pulled him to his feet and let him fold her into a hug, absorbing her sobs. They stood like that a while. Then she took a breath and he put a hand to her face.

"Don't let him go," he whispered. She shuddered. Remembering Blake's last words to her. Rob kissed her forehead and then tucked Lila under his other arm. Suzanne saw the swell of the other woman's belly. But instead of her usual quick spike of jealousy or resentment, she felt nothing but happiness for her friend. Rob reached into a cooler and grabbed some bottles of Blake's Brew, handed them out and raised his bottle.

She'd never felt more alone. Not after Mitchell's death. Not even when she'd forced Blake out of her life. She looked up through a haze of tears into Craig's dark brown eyes. He tugged her close and kissed her forehead as they raised their bottles.

The smell of the extra hoppy brew settled her stomach for a split second. Then, when it hit her palate, she had to hold back a gag. Putting a hand over her mouth, she stumbled towards the steps. Craig grabbed the bottle from her before she dropped it. "Sorry," she whispered, and ran up the steps and the rest of the group said their good byes.

She held onto the toilet, waited for her poor, overworked stomach to settle. She jumped at the sound of footsteps behind her. "

Lila stood, handing her a bottle of water. "Does he know?"

Suzanne wiped her lips, splashed water on her face. "Does who know what?" She groaned and closed the toilet lid to take a seat since there was no way she could stay on her feet. Lila crouched next to her and put a hand on her knee.

"Craig. Does he know you're pregnant?"

Suzanne frowned at the other woman. She'd blurted that very thing out to Craig's brother and sister-in-law, but the problem was her period had always been wonky. Not to mention that she was forty years old. She figured it was peri-menopause combined with the damage Mitchell had inflicted on her.

Her head pounded, which brought on another bout of nausea. She gripped Lila's hand. Stared into the woman's dark eyes. "I can't be."

Lila squeezed her knee and handed the water over. "I'll bring you some sliced lemon. It's the only thing that helps me."

Suzanne stared at her departing back. Her brain refused to process the possibility. She remembered the last time she and Craig had sex. In the pool. Almost two months ago. She grabbed the wall to keep herself steady.

Lila came back and handed Suzanne a sliced lemon. "Smell it. Trust me."

Suzanne stared at it. Put it to her nose, took a long breath, then took a sip of water. She felt Lila's eyes on her. She did it again. For the first time in weeks, she didn't feel mortally ill just standing and breathing air. "Oh God. That is amazing."

"Yeah. So, you gonna tell him, or what?"

Her eyes welled again. She brushed the tears away. She was angry, frustrated at her too little too late, pregnant, in her forties and alone self.

"Why? He doesn't want me anymore."

Lila let her sob it out, then looked at her. "Tell him."

"Tell him what?" Suzanne yelped at the sound of Craig's voice. Lila patted her cheek, then walked out. Suzanne stared at him. His dark stare, handsome face, so close. Yet so far from her.

"Nothing." She brushed past him.

But he grabbed her arm. "Talk to me."

The house was empty. She could hear childish laughter, lower adult voices, subdued but yet somehow celebratory, as it should be. She sank to the saggy couch, her face in her hands. Craig stood quiet. Terror grabbed her heart, made her breathless. The nausea rose again. She gripped her lemon, never more unsure of herself.

A baby. Holy shit.

But she must have waited too long.

"Never mind." He walked out, and she heard his motorcycle fire up. The squeal of tires signaled something final. She sighed, stood, stared around the empty room, and found a picture of Blake on the mantel. Her heart caught in her throat. She took it down, ran her finger over the image of his eyes, so green and expressive. His laughing face, caught in a candid happy moment, on one side of Lila, Rob on the other. She barely choked back a sob, sank to the couch and let the sounds of her friends and the laughter of children lulling her into an exhausted sleep.

She woke with a start, disoriented and dry mouthed. The room was pitch black. But the distinct sound of an unhappy toddler broke the silence.

She wandered into the hall and saw Brandis, Jack and Sara's near three-year-old son standing in the hall, whimpering, thumb stuck in his mouth. Suzanne knelt down, and he leapt into her arms, almost knocking her over.

"Sh... it's okay." She patted his back, stuck her nose into his neck and sucked in a breath of his little boy scent. He calmed, but kept his arms wrapped around her neck. She dropped onto the couch, making soothing noises as he hiccupped himself to sleep. She sat long into the night pondering options and possibilities, his little boy warmth soothing her.

At some point, Jack wandered out of his room and pulled a quilt over the two of them, waking her. She smiled at him, then fell back asleep. The little boy curled himself into her, keeping one arm wrapped tight around her neck.

Her dreams were a tangle of babies, and Craig. She woke when Brandis climbed across her and dropped to the floor, calling for his mommy. She sat, and did her pilgrimage to the bathroom, losing what few cookies she had.

Chapter Twenty-three

Craig glanced at his watch and grabbed a coat and tie, hoping he wasn't too late. Rob and Lila were getting married today, and the main reason he was going was because he knew Suzanne would be there.

He'd spent the last month in complete turmoil. Going from work to home to the pool to bed, then repeating the process. Avoiding everyone and everything that would remind him he was human. He felt like a goddamned robot. But it was all he could do. Anything else implied he'd allow himself to admit what he suspected about Suzanne.

He pulled up to the small chapel on the University of Michigan campus, snagging Katie when she dashed by in full fancy wedding sundress playing tag with her brother and cousins. He gave her a hug.

He approached Jack and Evan, looking around for Suzanne. His heart pounded. He was sweaty, nervous. Not himself at all. He shook Jack's hand, greeted Evan and the daughter who clung to him. Damn place was like a daycare center there so many kids.

"Thought I was late." He turned, almost choking on his own spit when he saw her slipping out from a side door of the chapel.

Her face was flushed, her hair blew around in the light breeze. It lifted the edge of her sundress when she slid her sunglasses down her nose. When he ducked out of sight, wanting to just watch from a distance without her seeing him, Jack leaned into his ear, startling him.

"There was a time when I had to be told to get the fuck over myself to get what I wanted." Craig never took his eyes off the woman he loved. "Go, doc. Go to her. Cut the shit and man-the-fuck up. She needs you. More than ever."

He turned, but Jack nodded towards the red-headed woman still standing in the chapel's shadow. She stepped out onto the grass. Her body seemed fuller than usual. Her face looked different. She put a hand on her stomach, a gesture that twanged every single one of his nerve endings. He swallowed hard. Told himself to move, to put one foot in front of the other, forward motion. Towards her.

She still hadn't seen him. He moved fast, caught her in his arms and tugged her back into the shadows.

"Hey!" She struggled for a second and then looked up into his eyes. At that moment, he knew.

He put a hand on her belly. She was so slight, he already felt the subtle change there. His ears buzzed, but he tried to keep cool. She squirmed, looked away.

"Suzanne," he whispered, brushed his lips over hers, relishing everything about her. Fear of the facts—an older woman, medically compromised, carrying a child. His child. He held onto her, forcing terror at her tenuous condition down under a solid layer of longing. She clung to him, went up on her tiptoes, and kissed him before he could say anything else.

She broke away, cradled his face in her hands. "Marry me?" she asked. "Please?" Her voice shook. Her entire body trembled. "I love you. I need you. I..." She put her hand over the one he had pressed to her stomach.

He stepped back, stared hard at her. "This is you asking me, huh?"

She nodded. He looked up, studied the movie-set blue sky. "I like the idea of that, Suzanne." He began. "But...."

She put fingers over his lips, making him wince with the effort to not kiss her again. "You know better than anyone that me being pregnant isn't a good idea."

He shoved his hands in his pockets, recalling stats and facts about the danger of having a child late in life, wondering how stable she could be during a pregnancy. But he lifted his chin. "What are you saying? You want me to make some kind of choice for you? As your doctor?" He let the unsaid words drift between them. "As the baby's father?" die on his lips.

She stiffened, took a step back. He knew the look that dropped into her eyes, veiling her newfound openness. The withdrawal had begun.

He tried not to let anger fill the space in his chest that she'd created months ago by rejecting him. But then, something happened. She swallowed, and her eyes filled with tears. The strong-as-steel, petite, beer-selling dynamo seemed to crumple right in front of him. "Craig, I'm s-s-s-scared."

He took a step towards her, his need to have her in his arms so strong he had to bite the inside of his cheek to stop himself.

"Don't be. Nothing bad will happen." He tried to summon his best doctor voice. He ran a finger down her wet cheek. When he spoke, his voice broke. "I won't let it. I promise. I won't let anything bad happen to you—ever." He held her, kissed her hair. "And yes, I will marry you, Suzanne."

Six Months Later

Craig stared at the monitor and steeled himself. "Honey." He put her icy hand to his lips. "We have to take her."

"No." Suzanne shook her head, her damp hair whipping around her face. She sucked in a breath when another contraction gripped her. "Ow. You promised me, Craig. You told me it would be okay."

He shoved down the urge to yell, knowing he had to stay calm, that he only had a few minutes to save his daughter's life. Suzanne had been so irrational about this option for a week, and it was about to cost him his child.

"It will, my love." He brushed her hair off her forehead. Kissed her, then motioned for the nurse. "Get Doctor Lane. Now."

He pulled Suzanne close, held onto her while the team around them leapt to action, draping her lower body with blue paper. The last few months had been a blur, simultaneously exciting, horrific, and terrifying. While most of him was glad she'd be getting the child she wanted, he spent a lot of time furious with himself for letting it get this far.

Between gestational diabetes and pre-eclampsia, she'd spent the bulk of the time flat on her back, anxious and antsy and making everyone's life miserable. Which turned him into a walking, talking, man-shaped bundle of tension and worry. They'd made it about four weeks past their small wedding before it all went bad and her body starting rejecting the pregnancy.

"Ow!" she yelped. His heart pounded, but he put a soothing hand to her face. "It hurts," she said, her voice hoarse. "She's okay, right? Promise me?"

"Sh..." he soothed and looked up. The head of the hospital's OB department had been with them from the start. The guy was good, better than good, and right now his expression was serious as he focused on his task.

A neonatal incubator appeared. The baby, a daughter, they knew, would be eight weeks premature, but her heart had almost stopped this morning while Suzanne groaned her way through yet more early contractions. So, despite all the risks, he agreed with the OB and the chief pediatrics. They had to get her out, now.

He closed his eyes, willing the nightmare away. "Oh," he heard Suzanne's voice, breathy and a little nervous. He looked up and saw Dr. Lane holding the tiny, quiet infant in his hands.

The nurse took her and tucked her into the incubator, hooking her up to a million leads, giving her all the usual checks and shots. Craig's throat contracted at the look in the man's eyes as he closed. The peds guy rushed in and gave the impossibly small baby a once over.

"Craig. Talk to me." Suzanne hadn't let go of him. He looked down at their clenched hands. Their wedding rings glinted in the bright operating room light. "Can I see her? Please?"

"Hang on." He kissed her, pried his fingers away, and took a couple of shaky steps to the plastic unit. His daughter stared up at him, her fists clenched, her mouth open, her skin turning a healthy pink as she sucked air into her small lungs. He gulped, put a hand on the top of the plastic. "Please," he croaked, and felt a tear slip down his face. "Lillian Grace. Please be okay."

The pediatric team was fussing around on the other side of the baby's unit. The department chief put a hand on his shoulder. "It's amazing Craig. She's in great shape. We'll keep her in this, of course, and use the feeding tube for a day or two. But, have Suzanne use the breast pump. The baby needs mama's milk to keep her strength up."

"Can I... can she hold her?" He put both shaking hands on the incubator, itching with the need to hold his child.

The guy shrugged. "She's pretty stable. I don't see why not." The nurse rolled the incubator close to Suzanne's bed, wrapped the girl in a blanket, and put her in his arms.

When Craig handed their small, beautiful girl baby to his wife, her eyes were dry. But his most definitely were not.

Epilogue

Fifteen Years Later

Suzanne stretched out in the lounge chair, hiding behind a giant hat, sunglasses, and tons of sunscreen. She studied the amazing array of children that splashed in Lake Michigan. Sara stood beside the chair, bearing Bloody Mary's for everyone. Jack ran by, kicking a soccer ball along the beach, followed by Rob and a group of adults and kids ranging in age from seven to twenty-three.

"Quite the crowd, isn't it?" Sara yelped when her husband smacked her ass on the way past. She sat, sipped, and held out a hand. Suzanne took it, held on tight. Craig ran up with a little boy on his shoulders. The child had a shock of stark black hair, light brown skin, and a smile that never faded.

Maureen, Jack's sister, joined the women. "You need more sunscreen, mister." She shielded her eyes up at the little boy who squealed when Craig dumped him onto the chair. Suzanne watched as he snuggled into his mother's arms. Blake, the youngest addition to their merry group, a seven-year-old miracle child most claimed, named by Jack's sister in honor of the one they had all lost. Everyone from adults to teenagers doted on him.

"I'm gonna jump into the match." Craig pointed down the beach where the adults and children had formed teams and were about to start a soccer game. Suzanne smiled at him as he trotted away.

Sara patted Blake's foot. He scrambled out of Mo's arms and leapt over to let his godmother lather the SPF fifty on him.

"Hey!" Jack yelled up at them. "Where's Brandis?"

Sara sighed, ignoring him and his question about their handsome, charming, eighteen-year-old son. She whispered to Suzanne. "I know. But I'm not telling him. Watch, give Rob about five seconds...."

They counted to five together. Rob's voice was next.

"Lila!" He yelled for his wife, who was instructing her little team before they started playing. "Where the hell is Blair?"

Lila looked up, shrugged, then resumed her mini-coaching session, not seeming to worry about the whereabouts of her sixteen-year-old daughter relative to Brandis' location. "Goddamn it, Gordon." Rob kicked the ball hard. Jack took it straight to the balls.

"Ow! Jesus Freitag. What?"

Suzanne's old friend, Sara's husband, groaned and tried not to grab his crotch. He glared at his friend, cupping himself while the kids fell out on the sand laughing.

Rob kept his eyes on Jack but hollered for his son. "Gabe. Go find your sister and get her the hell away from...."

Gabe held up a hand to stop his father's next words, nodded, and ran down the beach. He moved with the grace of a natural athlete as he loped past Suzanne, Mo, and Sara, who'd fallen out of their chairs giggling.

The recent discovery of Brandis and Blair in her room after his senior prom—by her father, who was supposed to be out of town—had led to no small amount of tension between the two men. They were old friends, but when it came to his daughter, Rob was more than a little protective and had been heard to say that "any son of Jack's" was not going near his daughter, which of course meant one thing.

"Mommy!" Blake squirmed away from Sara and bounded over to Mo, kissing her cheek. "I wanna play."

She held him tight a second. Suzanne looked up and saw a serious-looking teenager who could be Maureen's daughter with her jet-black hair and bright blue eyes. Sara smiled and held out her arm for a hug. The girl obliged her, then squirmed away.

"Mom, stop it. I just came to get Blakie for the game," she protested, until Sara sighed, kissed her hair, and let her go. She grabbed her cousin's hand.

Mo let go of the boy. "Go with Bethany. But make sure your dad remembers to..." Her voice faded when the two kids ran off without letting her finish.

Suzanne put her hand over her eyes to find her daughter. She spotted the girl's strawberry blonde hair first, smiling at the sight of her walking along behind Gabe as he hollered for his sister. A miracle herself, the only lasting issue she had from her premature birth was with her hearing, and she was scheduled for corrective surgery in a few weeks.

Suzanne let happiness surge through her as she watched Craig grab the girl and swing her around, making her screech with joy and terror. They both fell on the sand. Little Blake joined the girl and Bethany, helping bury Craig in the beach sand.

Suzanne knew her daughter was obsessed with Gabe, Rob and Lila's tall, handsome blond son and Brandis's longtime partner in crime. It worried her, but Gabe was a gentle and kind boy. He was calm, smart, athletic and best she could tell, the two of them were just friends.

For now.

It made Craig nuts, she knew, but he was coming to terms with the fact that his beloved daughter was growing up.

"I feel too blessed," she muttered.

Sara tapped her arm, nodded in the opposite direction from where Gabe had run, thinking to find his younger sister wandering around in the water, or reading, or drawing. Suzanne put her hand over her eyes. A couple was silhouetted on the promontory near the lighthouse. They sat close together, legs swinging over the side. Sara sighed when the boy lifted the girl's hand to his lips. Brandis and Blair, the young couple everyone was looking for at the moment.

"Here we go," Sara muttered. Suzanne patted her friend's arm, then returned her gaze to her family, her friends, her child, and to the love of her life.

The End

Aw, now wasn't that awesome? I loved giving those two their HEA!

Now it's time for you to know more about Evan Adams, Jack's friend who owns the other brewery in town. MUTUAL RELEASE is the next book in the series and it comes with a set of trigger warnings. Evan's backstory includes his growth into his natural, Dom personality. But it comes from experiences that show how BDSM can be misrepresented and used as abuse. Julie, the woman who becomes his sub and eventually his wife was sexually abused as a teenager. While none of the really bad stuff is shown on the page, her reaction to it is, and it forms the woman she becomes by the time she meets Evan.

MUTUAL RELEASE is a long novel, and also contains explicit BDSM scenes and situations. It's one of the books I am proudest of, as it allowed me to delve deep into two personalities that are almost as compelling in their own way and Jack and Sara. Oh and you'll also get a glimpse of early Jack Gordon from his days in law school and his first exposure to the BDSM lifestyle

* * * *

BY THE TIME SHE HUNG up, Julie felt like she had been through a wringer. She flopped back in her chair, tugged her shirt out of her ruined skirt, and unbuttoned her sleeves, her skin hot from the confrontation on the phone. Her feet ached and her calves were cramping up when she remembered she had skipped lunch.

"Paul! Go grab me a sandwich down the street, will ya? I need to stick here for at least another hour." She kicked off her shoes and started rubbing the arch of one foot.

"Hey." The voice she heard was most definitely not Paul's. It was the voice she'd been spending the better part of the past week trying to shove out of her head.

She shut her eyes, keeping her chair turned from the door and taking inventory of how wilted, coffee-stained, smelly she must be. But her skin pebbled, and a strange humming noise had started in her ears, which made her even madder and more inclined to ignore his sexy, low, bedroom voice.

"What do you want?" She thought about tucking her shirt back in, pulling her hair out of its lame ponytail and sticking her feet back in her shoes. For about three seconds. "My week-long silence not enough to convince you I'm not interested? I mean, in your brewery?" She willed him out of her office.

"I brought you something," he said.

She turned, her heart pounding so hard she thought he might see her shirt move.

"I don't want anything you have." Deciding to keep the whole conversation dialed to double entendre to show him she could handle it, she leaned on her desk, giving him a clear view of the tops of her D-cups down her shirt. But he kept his gaze pinned on hers. "Spare me the charm-fest, Adams. I'm immune. What is it? I'm busy."

"May I?" He pointed to the seat across from her desk.

She sighed and rolled her eyes. He took that as a "yes" and walked in. Evan Adams was dressed in a way she'd remember today—charcoal gray suit, accented by a deep blue shirt and identically colored tie. His black wingtips shone, and she noted with admiration the splash of brightness in the form of a snappy blue silk handkerchief in the suit pocket. Her knees shook. The man was, in a word, edible. But the look he shot her told her he knew it. And that brought a soothing, familiar bite of cynicism to her overwrought brain.

He plunked two six-pack carriers on her desk, one his, and the other emblazoned with none other than the Jackson Brewing Company's logo. She leaned over and pulled up bottles of each, noting there were three different types of beer from both his and Jackson's brewery in his offering.

"I'm not in the mood for a drink, but thanks anyway." She pushed back from the desk and put her bare feet on it, daring him to comment.

Her legs were bare and firm, and her skirt was short. To his credit, he didn't rise to her bait.

Keeping his eyes pinned to hers, Evan reached down and opened one of his, then one of Jackson's bottles. The tempting hops aroma filled the space between them. He set small empty plastic cups next to the sixers and poured some of each brew into two of the cups. She watched as he pushed them in front of her before leaning back, his gaze calm.

She raised an eyebrow at him, decided not to be obtuse, and tried first Jackson's, then the Big House version, which she had never tried. The difference was astonishing. But she wasn't about to let him know that.

"Okay, thanks for the taste test. You can go now."

"Hang on. Not done yet." He popped open the next two bottles, both classic American stouts, poured her a portion of each.

She frowned, shrugged and tasted those, coming to the same shocking conclusion. But she kept her face neutral, bored—although the longer he stayed in her space, the harder it was not to match his smile.

The final two brews were the most challenging: juicy IPAs, which in her opinion were trendy versions of the same-old, heavy-handed, over-hopped bullshit. Jackson's version was exactly that. But the balanced and less dense version from Big House made her sit up and take notice.

He leaned back, propped one ankle on the opposite knee, forcing her to recite an inner mantra to keep from looking straight at his crotch. She knew he was showing off what was a near-perfect male physique. But two could play at that little game.

She smiled, tugged her hair out of the holder and shook it, letting the waves cascade down her back and around her face. After rising to her feet, she took a few steps over to the large window overlooking a tidy courtyard.

The late October afternoon was easing towards evening, giving her the perfect angle of light. She held on to the last cup of beer, still marveling at its perfection, and turned, leaning against the ledge. Draining the last drops of the small sample, she made a noise that she knew damn well might pass for sexual pleasure and looked straight into his eyes.

"Impressive. I'll give you that. And ballsy, coming in here without an appointment to make me drink beer I didn't ask for." She allowed herself a moment to rake her eyes across his shoulders, down his torso, and right at his zipper.

He blinked, no longer sporting his Mr. Perfect grin. She put her hands on the ledge and leaned in again. The power bloomed in her once more, making her mad this time when his eyes fluttered down for a split second into the top of her blouse. The roaring, conflicted noise in her head kept deafening her as they stared at each other for a few seconds.

Julie had long buried any sort of honest sexual feelings. She reduced most men to their lowest common denominator pretty quickly, and she realized she was attempting to do that now, even though she knew she shouldn't. Evan had held his own, and she would have let it be, but for the vibe he was throwing—the one that addressed a long-buried sensation in her gut where a bizarre, melting feeling had taken up residence. She blinked and broke the contact first, sitting up and plucking the empty cup from the ledge.

But her knees shook as she tried to stay cool between window and chair. When her toe connected with a chair leg, she cursed. Unwanted tears welled in her eyes. She turned from him, blinking and trying to breathe.

"I'll take these samples to the staff tomorrow. Thanks," she said, waving a dismissive hand in his general direction and dropping into her desk chair. She clenched her jaw and stared into the setting sun, letting it burn circles into her retinas, hoping he would leave her to her misery.

Her toe throbbed like a motherfucker, and her head was pounding from lack of food plus afternoon alcohol. A hand on her knee made her jump.

To her utter shock and horror, Evan Adams was kneeling in front of her and had his hand on her foot.

"Let me see it," he said, his voice soothing instead of rattling her. Amazed at herself, she let go of her foot and allowed him to draw it into his lap. Wincing when he moved it, she yelped when he pressed on the red-painted nail. They both observed his hand moving to her ankle and up her calf. Julie leaned back and let him slide that hand up and up past her knee, gulping when he stopped under the edge of her coffee-fouled skirt.

He seemed as confused as she was to find himself up on his knees, his fingertips mere inches from her panties. A powerful shudder made her close her eyes, grip the arms of her chair as if in pain. It was painful, she mused, as this man who was a handsome be-suited total stranger leaned close, putting his full lips right next to hers.

Pulses of light and energy shot across her vision. When he pressed closer, the distinct edge of cologne—nothing overpowering but definitely there—made her eyes fly open. This was not happening, not to her. Not with this man whom she sensed could not only rock her, but would also tear her heart into a million pieces before he was finished. The power in her shriveled, retreated to a corner, and a different sensation flooded her nerve endings.

His other hand was at her face, his thumb moving over her lips, making her part them. His scent hit her nose once more, triggering a visceral reaction at odds with the pleasant realization the man was about to kiss her.

"Open your eyes." His whisper curled against her ear like smoke. She shook her head, not remembering when she'd closed them. "Now, Julie. Look at me."

The surety of that voice compelled her as she fought it on reflex. He would not order her around like a...

The hand on her thigh tightened. She opened her eyes and was hit once more by the perfection of his face and the puzzled look she saw on it. She gripped the chair arms harder, because if she didn't, she'd have her hands on his afternoon-rough jaw. They froze in this awkward tableau. She reared back, him looming over her, his hand halfway up her skirt.

Julie gave herself a firm mental shake. As she put her trembling hands on his chest to push him away, he brushed her lips with his. Just enough. And now she really couldn't breathe. He went slowly, testing her resolve versus her need. The chair beneath her disappeared, the bright room darkened as she eased her lips open.

But that fucking cologne. It was subtle, but it swirled in her head nonetheless, making her dizzy and terrified. A weird claustrophobia enveloped her, and the dizziness morphed into nauseating fear.

This was not what she did. This was not part of her plan.

She propped her feet against his thighs and pushed the wheeled chair away from him, leaving him off-balance, teetering until he dropped to all fours, still staring at her with eyes that made her want to rip his goddamn suit off. She clenched her jaw, throat frozen with unsaid words.

He crawled toward her at some point and put his hands on hers that still white-knuckled the chair arms. "You okay?" His voice was hoarse. She kept her eyes shut a second. Then opened them when she was ready.

He was there, kissable, and too close again. She smiled, but kept her voice firm. "What the fuck do you think you're doing?"

He blinked and backed away from her, as if a veil dropped between them. His odd but beautiful hazel eyes clouded with something she thought could be anger. He stood, stepping back so fast he stumbled and almost fell over her wastepaper basket. She watched him in dismay as he ran his hands through his hair, buttoned his coat, mesmerized by a sudden drop of sweat that appeared at his temple.

Dear Lord, but she wanted to lick it off.

And I know that you're going to want the rest of this series, like right now so here are some handy links to the rest of the Stewart Realty Saga:

Floor Time
Sweat Equity
Closing Costs
Dual Agency
Escalation Clause
Conditional Offer
Mutual Release
Backup Offer
PLUS the Jack Gordon Prequel: HOUSE RULES!

And don't miss GOOD FAITH—a Stewart Realty series affiliated novel that is an epic leap into the second generation. It is not a romance but it contains several romantic storylines.

· · · ·

IF YOU SUBSCRIBE TO my newsletter, you'll get all the awesome updates that I have planned for the coming year, including multiple novellas from this series, some of which you can ONLY get if you are a Liz Newz Subscriber!

Go to lizcrowe.com to subscribe.

And be sure to snag your free Stewart Realty Prequel: HOUSE RULES when you subscribe! This is EXCLUSIVE to Liz newsletter subscribers only!